Rightfully His

SHARON DE VITA

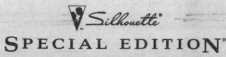

SPECIAL EDITION

Published by Silhouette Books

America's Publisher of Contemporary Romance

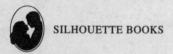

SILHOUETTE BOOKS

ISBN 0-373-24656-0

RIGHTFULLY HIS

Copyright © 2004 by Sharon De Vita

Visit Silhouette Books at www.eHarlequin.com

Printed in U.S.A.

Max had been halfway in love with Sophie from the moment both he and his twin brother, Michael, had laid eyes on her almost ten years ago.

But he knew immediately, Sophie was a woman who wanted roots and stability, a home and a family—the kind of security and stability that his vagabond photojournalist career and lifestyle simply wouldn't and couldn't provide.

So, he'd buried his own feelings and stepped aside, playing the role of the indulgent, protective big brother and leaving the path clear for his calm, staid, stable twin brother, Michael, who'd married Sophie less than a year later.

But Michael had been dead for almost three years now, leaving Sophie a widow and his nieces fatherless.

And if the girls' message was correct, apparently Sophie was finally over her grief and heartache, and quite ready to love and perhaps even *marry* again. But if Sophie thought he was going to step aside again and let some stranger become a father to *his* beloved biological daughters, well, she was mistaken.

The time had finally come for Max to claim what was rightfully his.

Dear Reader,

It's hard to believe that it's *that* time of year again—and what better way to escape the holiday hysteria than with a good book…or six! Our selections begin with Allison Leigh's *The Truth About the Tycoon,* as a man bent on revenge finds his plans have hit a snag—in the form of the beautiful sister of the man he's out to get.

THE PARKS EMPIRE concludes its six-book run with *The Homecoming* by Gina Wilkins, in which Walter Parks's daughter tries to free her mother from the clutches of her unscrupulous father. Too bad the handsome detective working for her dad is hot on her trail! *The M.D.'s Surprise Family* by Marie Ferrarella is another in her popular miniseries THE BACHELORS OF BLAIR MEMORIAL. This time, a lonely woman looking for a doctor to save her little brother finds both a healer of bodies and of hearts in the handsome neurosurgeon who comes highly recommended. In *A Kiss in the Moonlight,* another in Laurie Paige's SEVEN DEVILS miniseries, a woman can't resist her attraction to the man she let get away—because guilt was pulling her in another direction. But now he's back in her sights—soon to be in her clutches? In Karen Rose Smith's *Which Child Is Mine?* a woman is torn between the child she gave birth to and the one she's been raising. And the only way out seems to be to marry the man who fathered her "daughter." Last, a man decides to reclaim everything he's always wanted, in the form of his biological daughters, and their mother, in Sharon De Vita's *Rightfully His.*

Here's hoping every one of your holiday wishes comes true, and we look forward to celebrating the New Year with you.

All the best,

Gail Chasan
Senior Editor

Please address questions and book requests to:
Silhouette Reader Service
U.S.: 3010 Walden Ave., P.O. Box 1325, Buffalo, NY 14269
Canadian: P.O. Box 609, Fort Erie, Ont. L2A 5X3

Books by Sharon De Vita

SHARON DE VITA,

a former adjunct professor of literature and communications, is a *USA TODAY* bestselling, award-winning author of numerous works of fiction and nonfiction. Her first novel won a national writing competition for Best Unpublished Romance Novel of 1985. This award-winning book, *Heavenly Match*, was subsequently published by Silhouette in 1985. With over two million copies of her novels in print, Sharon's professional credentials have earned her a place in *Who's Who in American Authors, Editors and Poets* as well as the *International Who's Who of Authors*. In 1987, Sharon was the proud recipient of *Romantic Times*'s Lifetime Achievement Award for Excellence in Writing.

Sharon met her husband while doing research for one of her books. The widowed, recently retired military officer was so wonderful, Sharon decided to marry him after she interviewed him! Sharon and her new husband have four grown children, five grandchildren and currently reside in the Southwest.

Chapter One

"Hi, you've reached the voice mail of Max McCallister. If it's still October, then I'm out of the country on assignment. If it's not October, then I have no idea where I'm at, so just leave your name, number and a message, and I'll return your call as soon as I hit the States again. Thanks."

Six-year-old identical twins Carrie and Mary McCallister sat huddled on the floor, giggling as the sound of their beloved uncle Max's voice filled their bedroom.

"Hi, Uncle Max," Carrie shouted, leaning closer to the telephone which they'd dragged into their bedroom from the hallway. They'd decided to put the phone on the carpeted floor between them so they could both talk. "It's me, Carrie." Quickly, she passed the receiver to her sister.

"And me, Mary." Mary made her own voice just a tad louder than her sister's, as was her right, she figured, since she *was* the oldest of the twins.

"You said we could call you sometime," Carrie said with a slight frown, crossing her legs and leaning against her bed as she and Mary juggled the receiver between them.

"You said we could call *any*time," Mary corrected, crossing her own legs and scooting closer to her sister so they could both talk and listen. "So we're calling."

"Are you coming home for Thanksgiving?" Carrie asked.

"Cuz we haven't seen you in a long, long time," Mary added with a loud sigh, leaning her shoulders against her sister's bed.

"Yeah, Uncle Max, it's been a *reallllly* long time. And we miss you."

"Lots."

"We each lost our front tooth, Uncle Max."

"Yeah, and we both got silver stars on our spelling quiz."

"Grandma's taking tango lessons from Mr. Rizzo next door."

"And Mama's got a boyfriend," Carrie added,

rolling her eyes toward her sister. "His name is Mr. Beardsley. He's the vice principal at our school."

"Yeah, but all the kids call him Mr. Bugs-bee, Uncle Max, cuz he looks like a big ole bug," Mary finished with a giggle. "He's got these big pink lips that look like big fat raw hot dogs sitting on his face."

It was Carrie's turn to giggle. Determined not to be outdone, she launched into her own description of their current nemesis.

"Yeah, Uncle Max, and Mr. Bugs-bee's got real hairy black eyebrows that look like fat creepy spiders crawling across his forehead." Carrie shuddered. "Especially when he makes his mean face."

"And he makes his mean face at us. *A lot,*" Mary added with a scowl. "Especially when Mama or Grandma's not around."

"Yeah, Uncle Max," Carrie said, reaching up on her bed to grab her favorite doll and hugging it close. "And when Mr. Bugs-bee makes his mean face at us, his eyes get all big and buggy behind his glasses—"

"So that's why the kids call him Mr. Bugs-bee," Mary finished, collapsing on the floor in a fit of giggles.

"We don't think he likes us," Carrie said, glancing at her sister, who nodded in agreement, then lifted her chin defiantly.

"But that's okay, cuz we don't think we like

him,'' Mary said as she crossed her arms across her chest and looked at her sister for confirmation. ''Do we?''

''Uh-uh.'' Slowly, Carrie shook her head, sending her sable hair flying around her face. ''He's scary, Uncle Max,'' Carrie added.

''Yeah, Uncle Max, *real* scary. And once he even yelled at Carrie.''

''Yeah, Uncle Max, he yelled at me *real* loud. I hit his car with my volleyball.'' Carrie glanced at her sister and shivered again, hugging her doll closer. ''It was an accident. Honest. I didn't do it on purpose,'' she said defensively.

''We don't like him, but Mama does. Grandma says hi and to tell you she thinks Mr. Bugs-bee might be *the one*. We don't know what that means, but we don't think him being *the one* is anything good. Do you? Can you call us sometime, Uncle Max, and let us know if you're coming home for Thanksgiving?'' Mary said.

''Mama's making a big ole turkey and sweeter potatoes—''

''And devil's eggs and punky pie.''

''But Grandma said she's just going to make trouble cuz that's more fun and we're gonna help. So let us know if you're coming home, could you?'' Carrie asked.

''Bye, Uncle Max. We love you.''

''Yeah, Uncle Max, we love you. Call us!''

* * *

One week later...

Scowling, Max McCallister grabbed his drink, and gingerly stepped over his still-packed bags to press play on his answering machine.

The moment he heard the twins' voices fill his barren living room, he grinned, sinking his sore, aching body down carefully in his favorite chair.

As a war correspondent and photojournalist, he'd been in Iraq taking pictures for a national magazine for almost two months. Then, the past month had been spent in an overseas hospital, recovering from several gunshot wounds. He hadn't seen or talked to the girls since before he'd left. It wasn't until he heard their voices that he realized how much he'd missed them.

And their mother, Sophie.

Rubbing a hand over his stubbled beard, Max sipped his drink and let the girls' cheerful voices wash over him, trying not to think of Sophie.

He'd been halfway in love with Sophie from the moment both he and his twin brother Michael had laid eyes on her almost ten years ago. But he knew immediately that Sophie, beautiful, fiery, hot-tempered Sophie was a woman who wanted roots and stability, a home and a family. She wanted the kind of security and stability that his vagabond career and lifestyle simply wouldn't and couldn't provide.

So, he'd buried his own feelings and stepped aside, playing the role of the indulgent, protective big brother and leaving the path clear for his calm, staid, stable twin brother, Michael, who'd married Sophie less than a year later.

But his brother Michael had been dead for almost three years now, leaving Sophie a widow, and the girls fatherless—something that none of them had ever considered.

He'd gone to Chicago to help Sophie after Michael's death, of course, but fearing he might not be able to control his own feelings for Sophie, feelings that had nothing whatsoever to do with *brotherliness,* he'd left, not wanting to add any further to her heartbreak or her grief. Since then, he'd only gone back to visit for a few days at a time, fearing he wouldn't be able to hide his growing attachment to Sophie. His feelings were complicated by guilt as well as the fact that their relationship had never been simple. And that, he thought, taking a sip of his drink, was an *understatement.*

But if the girls' message was correct, apparently Sophie was finally over her grief and heartache, and quite ready to love and perhaps even *marry* again.

The thought had Max scowling.

Perhaps, he thought, the time had finally come for him to claim what was rightly his. A vision of the twins flashed in front of his eyes and something soft and warm gripped his heart. Yep, he decided, it was definitely time.

For his brother's sake, he'd stepped aside once to clear the way for Michael with Sophie. Then, for the girls' sake and Michael's he'd stepped away again when the twins were born.

When he'd learned his brother was sterile and he agreed to become a sperm donor, he never dreamed one day his brother might die, and a stranger could raise his beloved daughters.

So if Sophie McCallister thought he was going to step aside *again* and let some stranger become a father to his beloved *biological* daughters, well, *this time* Sophie McCallister was sadly mistaken!

"Girls, I mean it, this is your last warning." Annoyed, Sophie McCallister stood at the bottom of the living-room staircase, glaring up toward her twin daughters' bedroom on the second floor. "It's almost ten o'clock at night. You should have been asleep hours ago."

Feeling a bit embarrassed, Sophie flashed a wry smile at James Beardsley who was patiently sitting on the couch, waiting for her to finally get the girls settled down so they could have some privacy and some dinner.

"Now stop that giggling and whispering and go to sleep," Sophie ordered, trying to make her voice sound firm. ''Or no movie or pizza tomorrow night.''

Helplessly, she glanced at James again, feeling just a bit sorry for him. This dating business was new to her, and clearly not the quiet, romantic Friday evening dinner James had obviously planned.

A cozy fire blazed in her living-room fireplace, and the lamps had been dimmed and flickering candles provided a soft golden aura of romance. An array of cold appetizers and her fresh, homemade Italian hors d'oeuvres were artfully arranged on the game table around the beautiful crystal vase of long-stemmed red roses James had brought her. To complement their meal, James had also brought along a very expensive bottle of French wine that now sat open on the table, just waiting for them to enjoy.

The table was set, the atmosphere was cozy and romantic, but so far, they hadn't actually had a moment to do anything more than chaperone her two rambunctious daughters and try to get them settled down for the night.

And Sophie wasn't quite certain if she was annoyed—or relieved.

She wasn't totally convinced she was ready for the dating game again. As a thirty-year-old widowed single mother, she had enormous responsibilities and at times felt old beyond her years; far older than most of her peers, most of whom were just starting their careers and their marriages, while she'd already married and buried a husband, given birth to twins, and had still somehow managed to carve out a satisfying teaching career.

But she'd explained her familial obligations and responsibilities to James *before* she'd reluctantly accepted his offer to begin seeing him on something more than a professional basis, she reasoned, flashing him another small, nervous smile.

James was the vice principle of the school where she taught and he was kind, blond, balding, and totally nonthreatening, which was why she'd specifically agreed to go out with him.

As she traversed this new path of male-female relationships, she certainly didn't want to add pulse-pounding lust to the mix, since that would not only complicate things, but quite frankly, would scare her to death. Dating again was intimidating enough without having to worry about any added stress.

Besides, she was still nervous about mixing business with pleasure. But after being alone for three years, and after listening to her mother's nagging for most of that time—telling her it was more than *past* time for her to join the living once again—Sophie realized perhaps it *was* time to dip her toe back into the dating pool, if only to ease some of the enormous loneliness she'd felt since the girls' birth.

Then of course, she thought with a weary sigh, brushing back her tumble of black curls, there was the added advantage of getting her mother off her proverbial back.

So she was thinking of this dating thing as more of an adult version of a science experiment, rather than a stepping-stone into a wild and wicked adventure.

She wasn't an adventuresome kind of woman, preferring home and hearth to hot spots and hit parades.

She'd been perfectly honest with James, clearly explaining that this was a trial dating situation, a way for her to see if she was even ready to step back into that world again.

James, in his usual patient way, had claimed he understood that dating a single mother of twin girls had its pitfalls, but he was certain he could handle it.

Tonight, they were clearly putting his understanding to the test.

"I'm running out of patience, girls," Sophie added as the doorbell rang. She cast a quick, guilty glance at James, wondering how he felt about this unpredictable aspect of her life.

With her mother living with her, and twin six-year-old girls, not to mention a menagerie of strays the girls and her mother were forever bringing home—both the four-legged and two-legged kind— her house more often than not resembled a three-ring circus rather than the carefully polished and perfect home she was certain a man like James was accustomed to.

When the doorbell rang again, James offered to get the door. "I'll take care of this matter," he said with authority, smoothing down his tie, and then the jacket of his expertly cut suit. "It's far too late to be receiving visitors," he added with a frown as he headed toward the door. The bell rang again just as he got there.

When he opened the door, he froze, staring at the disheveled man who lounged in the doorway, holding onto a scarred, scruffy leather duffel bag.

"Oh my word," James finally stammered, blinking hard behind his owlish glasses. "I...I...I thought...I thought you were..."

"Dead? Sorry to disappoint you, pal, but you've got the wrong McCallister brother. I'm Max, not Michael," he said, sweeping efficiently past the still-shaken James and into the living room. "Sophie!" Grinning hugely, Max dropped his duffel bag and headed toward her.

"Max." Sophie felt her heart tumble over in one quick movement. "Oh my God, Max, what on earth are you doing here?" she asked in delight as he crossed the room in three strides and grabbed her in a huge hug, twirling her around.

At thirty-five, Max was the kind of man who wore his age well, growing more distinguished every year. His eyes, deep, dark-blue and so much like his late brother's and her daughters' eyes, were fringed with inky black lashes that even a supermodel would envy.

At six-five, Max never had the gawkiness that some tall men possessed. Instead, his body was lean and rangy, yet filled out in all the right places. He had an air of confidence that all but radiated through any room he entered, drawing people to him like a bee to a pot of honey.

Max had the kind of rough-hewn, recklessness that filled women's darkest sexual fantasies. With his thick, wavy black hair, his scruffy, careless elegance, and his penchant for adventure and danger he was what Sophie's mother had always called a "bad" boy, the kind of man who'd simply scared Sophie to death with his reckless desire to live every moment of life as if it were his last.

Toss that gorgeous recklessness together with an abundance of charm that covered an endless well of kindness and confidence, and you had a man who had made more than a few female hearts skip a beat.

Including hers.

Dear Max, she thought, as she wrapped her arms tightly around him and just held on, allowing herself to savor him and the moment.

Over the years since she'd married his late brother, Max had become her best friend, her big brother, her protector and above all the person in the world she trusted more than anyone else.

As usual, she hadn't heard from him in three months. Except for an occasional postcard or a late-night call to the girls.

But that was Max, never staying in one place long enough for even his shadow to fall, and she'd gotten accustomed to it. She appreciated him when he was here, but understood—and expected it when he left.

"I'm so glad to see you," she said, as he set her back down on her feet. Delighted, she lifted her hands to cradle his face. "We've missed you so much," she said, blinking away tears with a laugh. It was silly to cry, she knew, but where Max was concerned she was more than sentimental. He'd unselfishly given her the ultimate gift, and there was nothing in the world she wouldn't do for him.

"What are you doing here?" she asked, planting her hands on her hips. "And why didn't you tell us you were coming? I thought you were on assignment somewhere in the Middle East?"

An award-winning, world-famous photojournalist, Max leapt from one international hot spot to another in pursuit of his career.

"I was, Sophie," Max said with a grin, unable to conceal his joy at seeing her. She looked terrific, as usual. "But I decided to come home for a while. And if I'd told you, it would have ruined the surprise, now wouldn't it?" Holding her at arm's length, he drew back. "Now let me look at you."

His gaze greedily drank her in, roaming from the top of her glossy black head to the tips of her high-heeled boots.

She looked more like a teenager than a mother. With her petite curvy frame, and her long, curly dark hair, the large, intense eyes that were more black than brown, and that full, lush mouth glistening with something that all but begged a man to taste her. He could feel a mixture of lust and love mingle inside, nearly dizzying him.

Unable to resist, he slid his arms around her waist again, letting his gaze meet hers for one, long breath-stealing moment.

"You look terrific, Sophie," he said with a grin, drawing her even closer until they were toe to toe, body pressed against body, sharing warmth and heat. "Absolutely terrific. But then again, you always do," he added in a voice meant only for her ears.

Sophie shivered, lifting her hands to his broad chest to steady herself as his deep, masculine voice slithered over her, making every nerve ending spring to life.

Standing so close to him, his masculine heat warmed her, while his scent teased and delighted her, filling her with longing. She was reminded for the first time in a long time that she was a young, healthy woman.

Shaken at the impact Max still had on her, even

after so long, Sophie struggled to control her emotions, tilting her head to meet his intense gaze.

"Max." Her voice trembled out of her. Her body was reacting in a way that was sending alarm bells ringing through her brain. She knew better than to allow her feelings to run rampant where Max was concerned. But a woman could yearn, she thought giddily.

"I missed you, Sophie," Max whispered, ignoring the warning he read in her eyes and letting his gaze settle on that lush, lovely mouth of hers, a mouth that had haunted his nights and his days for as long as he could remember. "All of you."

Instinctively, she pressed her hands to his chest to try to hold him at bay as he lowered his head toward her, his mouth just a heartbeat away. Her own heart began a wild, wicked gallop as her knees grew weak.

"Max," she whispered again, trying to drag up some defenses. Instead, the moment his mouth touched hers, a riot started in her heart and all her resolve melted.

Max kissed just like he did everything else—*well*, and Sophie found herself clinging to his shirt, her breath catching, her fingers fisted tightly in the material as his mouth dragged her someplace heady, dark and forbidden. A place that erased every coherent thought from her mind and stole every bit of strength and resistance she'd worked so hard to build over the years until all she could do was feel.

And it was glorious, Sophie thought with a sigh, wrapping her arms tightly around Max and kissing him back. Absolutely glorious. It had been years since she'd been kissed like this by a man.

Years since she'd allowed herself to feel this stunning array of emotions. And she reveled in them for the moment, forgetting herself and her own resolve to always keep her feelings for Max under control. All he had to do was touch her, and her heart sped up, her limbs went weak, and her pulse scrambled as if in a mad dash.

But she'd always known that in spite of her physical reaction to Max, emotionally she simply couldn't allow him to touch her heart. They were two different people with different wants, needs and lifestyles, and as much as she adored Max, she knew she couldn't change him. Nor would she want to.

So, she accepted him for exactly who and what he was—the kindest, most loving, generous man she'd ever met—but she'd always known he wasn't the man for her.

Sliding his hands over the soft material of the back of her sweater, Max sighed, taking the kiss deeper, bringing her still closer, trying to fill the ache and void in his heart that had always been there because of her.

Daydreams of her couldn't even come close to the

actuality of holding her in his arms again and kissing her. Feeling the softness of her body curve and curl sweetly against him. His heart kicked him hard, then spun recklessly out of control as her body shifted and she pressed tighter against him.

He heard a soft moan of desire, and realized it had come from him. He wanted Sophie. Now. Right here.

But he'd been controlling that want for so many years, it was like second nature to him now. Wanting and never having seemed to be the story of his life, he thought with a little sigh.

Not anymore, he thought firmly.

Max McCallister had finally come home to claim what was rightfully his.

"Max." Sophie whispered his name, then lifted her shaking hands to his broad chest, effectively pushing him away, but still clinging to his shirt with her fingertips for balance since her knees felt like limp linguini. "Wow." Sophie shook her head to clear it, and tried to remember who she was and what the heck she'd been doing before Max had kissed her senseless.

"Excuse me." The front door slammed shut with a bit more force than necessary, causing Max and Sophie to jump apart, then turn toward James.

Uh-oh.

Sophie flushed guiltily, glancing at Max. Apparently, lip-locking with your brother-in-law in the middle of your date with a new man was *not* considered proper etiquette if the look on James's face was any indication.

"James." With her voice not quite steady, Sophie took a deep breath, patted her still-fluttering heart and forced a smile. "I'd like you to meet Max McCallister, my brother-in-law. Max, this is Mr. Beardsley, the vice principal of the school where I teach."

"I'm James," Beardsley said, moving toward Max with his hand outstretched. "A very close friend of Sophie's. And the girls."

"So I've heard," Max said in a tone of voice that had Sophie narrowing her gaze on him.

Max took James's hand and shook it, squeezing it a bit harder than necessary. "The girls told me all about you," Max added in a voice he hoped the man would recognize as a warning.

"Did they now?" James asked. "You know how dramatic children can be."

"No, I don't," Max said, the smile never leaving his face as he released James's hand. "Why don't you tell me, Jim?" he added, then frowned as he glanced around the romantically lit room and the elegantly set table.

"It's James," Beardsley corrected stiffly.

Max scowled. "Why is it so dark and gloomy in here, Sophie? Did you forget to pay the electric bill?" Without waiting for an answer, Max moved around the room, blowing out candles and turning on lamps.

"There, that's better." Satisfied he'd dissolved any thought of romance, Max turned to James with a grin. "Now, you were just about to tell me something about the girls?" Max planted his hands on his hips in a stance destined to intimidate. "But let me give you fair warning, I'm very partial to those two little imps, and I don't imagine I'll take too kindly to criticism of them, but if you're willing to risk it…fire away," Max said with a deceptively calm smile.

Shifting nervously, James smiled hesitantly. "Yes, well…I've found them to be…delightful children," he said, his voice catching nervously.

"Oh really?" Max said with a lift of his brow as he crossed his arms across his chest. "That's not what I've been hearing."

"Max," Sophie hissed, giving him a poke in the back. "Behave yourself," she ordered. "James is my date."

"I thought this guy was just your boss," Max said in a tone of voice that had Sophie rolling her eyes.

She glanced at James.

Uh-oh.

"On the contrary," James retorted hotly. "Sophie and I are much more than employee and employer. Aren't we, dear?" he asked with a smile, not bothering to wait for Sophie's confirmation. "We've gotten quite close over the past few months,'' he added.

''Isn't there some kind of rule or law prohibiting that kind of fraternization between employees and their bosses?'' Max asked with a frown, glancing from James to Sophie, whose eyes widened in annoyance.

''Actually, there's not,'' James said, nervously smoothing down his shirt collar.

''Well then, maybe there should be,'' Max said cheerfully, causing James to stiffen.

''Our personal relationship is just that. *Personal*,'' James said. His tone of voice could have put frost on the vase of roses on the table, making it quite clear his relationship with Sophie was none of Max's business.

Amused, Max merely lifted a brow. ''Is that so?'' Spotting the open bottle of expensive French wine, Max reached for it and poured some into a wineglass on the table. ''Is this for something special?'' Max asked innocently, lifting the glass in the air to study the deep, maroon liquid, before quickly draining it in one long gulp that had James's pale face going even paler.

''Actually, that wine was to enjoy with our dinner,'' James said stiffly, and Max grinned.

''Great.'' Max pulled out a chair at the elegantly set table for two and sank into it, crossing his legs at the ankle and making himself comfortable. ''I'm starving. So, when do we eat?''

Chapter Two

James deliberately ignored Max's question about dinner. Instead he asked, "How long will you be staying, Max?"

"Oh, I don't know, for a while," Max said airily.

"A while," James repeated in disbelief, his eyes widening in alarm.

"Yes," Max said with a grin. "The girls invited me home for Thanksgiving and I thought I'd take them up on their offer."

"But Thanksgiving isn't for more than a month yet," James remarked.

Sophie tried to conceal her delight. The idea of Max being there for a month filled her with both joy and worry. Joy because her daughters would be thrilled, and worry because she wondered how she was going to keep her emotions in check with Max living under the same roof for so long.

But if she knew Max, that month would probably turn out to be only a few weeks. Staying too long in one place gave Max itchy feet, and she knew as soon as the ailment hit, he'd be out the door and gone before she could blink.

"Yes, I know," Max said to James with a grin and a shrug of his big shoulders. "But I had some time off so I thought I'd head back here to spend some time with the girls."

"Max, you're not hurt, are you?" Sophie asked worriedly, wishing James didn't look quite so delighted at the prospect. The only time Max came home for any length of time was when he was hurt and in need of recovery time.

"No more than usual," Max said with a careless wave of his hand. Wistfully, he glanced up the stairs. "I don't suppose the girls are still up?"

"Actually, we've finally just gotten them down for the night," James injected, annoying Max even further.

One dark brow lifted and Max found his resentment simmering, wondering where this guy got off using the term *we* when it came to the girls. *His* girls. "Really?"

"Yes, really," James said stiffly.

Max stood up, set his wineglass down, then walked to the bottom of the staircase. "Hey girls," he called in a voice loud enough to wake the dead. "You guys sleeping?" He laughed when he heard their squeals, then the pounding of little feet across the floor upstairs. "Guess they're not asleep after all," Max said with a shrug.

"Uncle Max! Uncle Max! You came home. You came home. We knew you would! We knew it!" Dressed in matching nightgowns, Carrie and Mary pounded barefoot down the stairs, launching themselves at him before they reached the bottom step.

He caught them both, wincing only slightly as his still taped ribs gave a groan of protest. With a twin in each arm, he hugged them tight, swinging them around in a circle until they were all dizzy.

"I missed you both so much," he said twirling them again and making the twins squeal in delight. "Look at you two," he said, setting them down on their feet. "You're almost all grown up." They giggled as they always did when he told them that, but it was true, at least it seemed so to him. They were growing up so fast, and he had missed so much of their lives.

Not anymore, he thought firmly, gathering both girls in his arms again for a long hug.

"I think your mother's been watering you at night just so you'd grow taller," he said with a grin, hugging the girls tightly to him as his empty heart filled with an overpowering love unlike anything he'd ever known.

It had been that way from the moment of their birth. He'd seen the twins moments after they'd been born and the feelings that had swelled at the sight of them had stunned and surprised him.

He never thought his lifestyle would allow for parenthood, nor did he ever think of himself as a paternal type of person which was why he'd agreed to this arrangement in the first place. He'd been certain it would do no harm to anyone.

It had been one of the rare moments of poor judgment in his life, one that he'd lived to regret.

Because from the moment he'd laid eyes on the girls, nothing had mattered except for the overwhelming sense of possessiveness, love and protectiveness he'd felt toward those two helpless, adorable little twins.

"How long are you gonna stay, Uncle Max?" Carrie asked.

"Yeah, Uncle Max how long can you stay?" Mary echoed her sister, openly glaring at Mr. Beardsley.

"Well, girls," Max said, standing up and taking each girl by the hand as he led them to the intimately set table for two. "I'm not sure, but I figure I'll be here until at least Thanksgiving." He glanced down at them. "You did invite me, remember?"

"Yippee!" the girls caroled in unison, jumping

up and down and clapping their hands as they hugged his legs, nearly toppling him. ''You'll be here for turkey day, then?''

''Absolutely.'' Max grinned as he pulled out a chair and helped the girls into it, reaching across the table to pop an olive in his mouth from the platter of cold, beautifully arranged appetizers in the middle of the table.

Wistfully, he glanced around. Everything in this house had Sophie's womanly touch, including this elegantly set table. She'd turned this ramshackle, run-down old farmhouse into a warm, welcoming home.

''Well, Sophie,'' James said, clearing his throat, then adjusting his tie. ''Perhaps it would be best if we postpone our plans for this evening.'' He glanced at Max and the girls, trying hard to hide his disdain. ''It seems as if this isn't a good time.''

''Oh James, I'm sorry, did we spoil your plans for the evening?'' Max asked with decided glee as he got to his feet. ''I'm sorry, really,'' he said with absolutely no sincerity, ''but I'm sure you can understand that it's been a long time since I've seen Sophie and the girls and we do have a lot of catching up to do.''

He grabbed the man's elbow and began hustling him toward the front door, barely allowing the man's perfectly polished shoes to touch the floor.

''I'm sure you understand, don't you ole boy?''

Max asked, still holding onto the man's elbow as he yanked open the front door.

Sophie stepped forward, glaring at Max as she tried to pry James loose from his grip. "Max, let me just see James to his car."

"Do that," Max said with a grin, as Sophie opened the closet door and reached for her coat. "I'll wait right here," he added, making it sound like a threat as he leaned against the open door where he had a clear view to the four-door sedan sitting at the curb.

In the darkness, a faint breeze kicked up and Max sniffed the cool, late October air, reveling in the brisk bite. He'd just come from the Middle East and had his fill of the intense, dry heat and the endless, barren desert.

Here in the Midwest though, fall was receding, the trees were all but bursting with beautiful fall leaves, and winter was in the air, nipping cold and crisp in the dark night with the promise of the first snow in the not-too-distant future.

Shivering in delight, Max ran his hands up and down his arms. He hadn't realized exactly how good it would feel to be home. He turned to Sophie, and felt another kick right in his heart. And home, the only home he'd ever known had always been here, with Sophie and the girls.

"It's getting cold out, Sophie," Max said, helping her on with her suede jacket. "So don't stay out too long. We wouldn't want you to catch cold now would we?'' He zipped her jacket up to her chin, effectively hiding every inch of her from James behind the thick suede barrier, then patted her shoulders in approval.

''Max,'' she growled at him under her breath, her annoyance at his overprotective behavior getting the best of her. ''I'll be right back.'' She turned to James with a small, forced smile. ''James?'' She slid her arm through his and stepped through the doorway, grabbing the doorknob to shut the door firmly behind her so that they'd be away from Max's prying eyes at least for a few moments.

''That was Mr. Bugs-bee,'' Mary said. ''The one we told you about on the phone.''

Max nodded. ''The one who yelled at Carrie, right?'' he asked.

''Yep.'' Carrie's dark head bobbed and her lower lip trembled. ''That's him, Uncle Max.'' Tears flooded her eyes and her lower lip began to tremble, nearly breaking his heart. ''He said I was undiss... undis...''

''Undisciplined,'' Mary supplied. ''He said we was spoiled and lacked...discipline.''

''Yeah well, the only thing spoiled around here are his dinner plans,'' Max said with a grin. ''And discipline is for the military.'' Max walked over to the table, sat down in the empty chair and reached for Carrie, pulling her into his lap to wrap his arms protectively around her. When she snuggled closer, he planted kisses atop her shiny black head. "Not for little girls, right?"

"Right, Uncle Max," Mary said firmly, lifting her chin defiantly.

He tilted Carrie's chin up so she met his gaze. "I promise you that Mr. Beardsley will never ever yell at you again, for anything."

"Really, Uncle Max?" Wide-eyed with awe and love, Carrie grinned in relief.

"Really," Max confirmed.

"We hoped you'd come home when you got our message," Mary said, poking a finger among the platter of appetizers. "Cuz we didn't know what to do about Mr. Bugs-bee."

"He doesn't like me, Uncle Max," Carrie said, her eyes filling, then spilling over again. "And I don't know why. No one has ever not liked me before."

"Shh, shh, now, baby, don't cry," Max soothed in a near panic. The sight of so many tears on such a small female was enough to send him into a tailspin. He couldn't bear the thought of the girls being hurt or unhappy, and his anger at James Beardsley intensified.

"It doesn't matter if Mr. Beardsley likes you or not, sweetheart," Max whispered, gathering Carrie tighter into his arms, not quite certain what to do next. "Mr. Beardsley doesn't matter at all." He planted soft, comforting kisses across her damp cheek and forehead.

Carrie's eyes widened as she looked up at him with absolute, total trust, a trust he knew he would never break.

"He doesn't?" she asked, blinking away her tears.

Max shook his head. "Nope, sweetheart, he doesn't matter at all." Grateful her tears seemed to have stopped, at least for the moment, Max leaned his forehead against Carrie's, his heart aching because he knew how unhappy she was. "We don't like him either," he said softly. "Right, Mary?" he asked.

Mary's dark head bobbed. "Right, Uncle Max." Happily, she turned her grin to her sister and shrugged. "We don't like the bug-man, Carrie, so who cares if he doesn't like us?"

"But I think Mama likes him, Uncle Max," Carrie said softly. She leaned closer so she could whisper in Max's ear. "Grandma thinks Mama's going to marry him," she confided. "And we don't want her to marry him."

"Did you tell your mother that?" Max asked, his glance going from one little girl to the other.

"Uh-uh," Carrie whispered. "We was afraid to."

"I wasn't afraid," Mary said bravely, lifting her chin in a way that reminded Max of himself at that age. "But I thought we'd better wait to tell Mama until you came home to help, Uncle Max, just in case.'' When he looked at her in confusion, she went on. ''Uncle Max, we're…not afraid of Mama, but I guess me and Carrie, we're kinda afraid of Mr. Bugs-bee,'' she admitted sheepishly.

''As long as I'm alive, girls, you never have to be afraid of anyone,'' he said firmly. He tilted Carrie's trembling chin up so he could meet her frightened gaze. ''You got it, sweetheart?'' Solemnly, she nodded, snuggling even closer to him. He turned to Mary. ''That goes for you, too, Mary. You guys don't ever have to be afraid of anything as long as Uncle Max is alive,'' he repeated. ''And as for your mother marrying Mr. Beardsley, well, pigs will fly first,'' Max said.

''But pigs can't fly, Uncle Max,'' Carrie said solemnly, her delicate brows folding into a frown of confusion.

Max chuckled. ''Exactly, sweetheart.'' Max nuzzled her neck, savoring her little-girl smell and making her squirm and giggle. ''And that's exactly when your mother's going to marry Mr. Beardsley.''

''That means never, Carrie,'' Mary explained with a giggle.

''Really?'' Carrie's eyes widened in relief. ''You're not going to let Mama marry the bugman?''

''Absolutely not,'' Max said just as firmly, then grinned at the girls.

"I love you, Uncle Max," Carrie said, wrapping her arms tighter around his neck.

"And I love you, too, baby," Max said, cradling her closer. He frowned suddenly. "Now, we just have to figure out how to get rid of him." Without letting Sophie know what they were doing, he thought, as the front door opened and she walked into the house.

"Max, do you want to tell me what is going on?" Sophie asked, slipping off her coat. "You show up out of the blue, Max, after three months, and claim you've come for the holidays, as if I'm supposed to believe that?" Sophie turned toward him, pushing up the sleeves of her sweater, trying to hang on to some anger. But the truth of the matter was she was grateful James had left. She couldn't remember when she'd been so nervous, and the fact was, she was glad to see Max. Even if his behavior had sent James screaming quickly into the night.

"I did come home for the holidays," he said innocently. "Right, girls?"

Twin ebony heads bobbed in unison. "Yeah, Mama, we asked Uncle Max to come home."

"You did," Sophie said, looking at her daughters carefully and trying to figure out if the three of them were in cahoots about something. If not, why did she suddenly feel as if she was being... bushwhacked?

"Yeah, Mama, we asked you if we could call

him. Remember, a few weeks ago? And you said yes,'' Mary reminded her as Sophie nodded.

''You're right, I forgot.'' She looked at Max again, wondering why she had this suspicious tickle at the back of her neck. It never failed to serve as an early warning sign when something was wrong.

''So what *is* for dinner?'' Max asked, popping an olive in his mouth and flashing Sophie a grin. ''I'm starved.''

Throwing up her hands, Sophie went to warm up dinner.

''Well, Sophie, it's nice to know some things never change,'' Max said. ''You still make the best damn lasagna I've ever tasted.''

''Thanks,'' she said with a smile, getting to her feet and clearing his plate. ''I'm just sorry James didn't get a chance to taste it as well,'' she said, giving him a look.

''Sophie.'' Amused, Max reached out and caught her arm. Her skin was so warm and soft, it sent a tingle all the way to his belly. Absently, his thumb caressed her skin. ''I'm sorry if I screwed up your plans for tonight,'' he said, trying to keep a straight face.

''No, you're not,'' she retorted with a laugh, looking at him and seeing the mischief dancing in his eyes. Once again, the back of her neck began to tingle and she wondered what was up.

"Yeah, well, I guess you're right." Max sighed. "You know I've never been very good at lying."

"I know, but thanks for trying," she said with a wry grin. "I guess it's just kind of hard to admit that at the ripe old age of almost thirty, I think I flunked my first date." Sophie sighed, then stacked the rest of the dirty dishes, before lifting them into her arms to take into the kitchen. "I'll put the coffee on."

First date? Max thought about that for a moment. From what the girls' message had said, he'd gotten the impression Sophie had been seeing Beardsley for a while.

But maybe they'd only been friends up until now. That gave him some encouragement. Maybe the situation wasn't as dire as he feared.

"Got any homemade cannolis out there?" Max called and she grinned. She hated to admit that she'd always loved cooking for Max. Perhaps because he'd always had a healthy male appetite, and more importantly, he had always appreciated her skills in the kitchen.

She'd given the girls a half an hour with Max, while she'd put the lasagna in the oven, then she'd shooed them back up to bed where they'd finally fallen asleep with the promise that Max would be there for a while, and they could spend the whole next day with him if they wanted.

He did totally outrageous things that never failed

to surprise, even shock her, and he said even more outrageous things, but all was done with a smile and a mischievous twinkle in his eyes, so how on earth could she ever get upset with him?

Now that he was home again, she was feeling particularly vulnerable once more. But she was going to try this time to keep her feelings and emotions under wraps, she thought firmly, grabbing several coffee mugs from the mug rack on the counter.

Because the last time Max had come home, she'd allowed herself to start wishing and longing, and then all those emotions had turned into a desperate yearning that had only become painful once Max had left—as he invariably did.

This time she'd be smarter.

She hoped.

When the coffee was done, she grabbed the platter of fresh cannolis she'd made this afternoon after school, some napkins, the empty mugs, and headed back into the living room.

Max had dimmed the lights once again, and relit the candles. The light from the candles, coupled with the soft, burning glow of the fireplace made the room seem warm and cozy and almost as romantic as it had been when Max had arrived.

A warning bell went off in Sophie's mind again, but she forced a smile and ignored it.

''I thought we could sit here to have our coffee and maybe get caught up on each other's lives. It has been awhile.'' He took the coffeepot from her and set it down on the table in front of him, along with the platter of pastries. ''Ahh, this is more like it,'' Max said, reaching for one of the cannolis and biting into it. ''Your cooking is so much better than the hospital's.''

''Hospital?'' Alarmed, Sophie sank down on the couch next to him. ''I knew something was wrong, Max. I knew it,'' she said with a shake of her head. ''You're hurt, aren't you, that's why you're home?''

''Sophie.'' Max sighed, sorry he'd ever let those words about the hospital slip. ''It's no big deal.''

''The last time you told me that someone had put two bullets in your limbs, remember?'' she reminded him with a scowl.

''Yeah, I remember, that was one helluva experience, though,'' he said with a grin. ''But I must admit I got some fabulous pictures out of that.''

''Terrific. You should be glad you're not taking pictures from a wheelchair.'' She took a deep breath before asking her next question, wanting to make sure she was prepared for the answer. ''Okay, Max, exactly how 'not a big deal' is it this time?''

He shrugged and continued eating, helping himself to another pastry, then sipping the coffee she'd poured for him.

''I just happened to wander into the middle of a firefight between two tribal leaders in a small Middle Eastern border town while trying to snap some photos.'' Regretfully, he shook his head as he set his cup down. ''They would have been great shots, too.''

''A *fire*fight?'' She frowned. ''Oh my God, do you mean people were *shooting* at each other and you got into the middle of it?''

He flashed her a charming smile that never failed to cause her pulse to scamper like a frightened rabbit. ''Yeah, that was about the gist of it.''

Absently, she laid a hand on his arm, feeling his masculine warmth through his shirt, making her nerve endings tingle. ''Okay, so if you got in the middle of this, did you get shot?'' she asked, pressing her free hand to her chest to take a deep breath.

''Yeah, I guess you could say that,'' he answered calmly, reaching for his third pastry. She slapped his hand away.

''No more cannolis until you tell me the truth, and nothing but the whole truth.'' Trying to look firm, she crossed her arms across her breasts. ''Now.''

Max sighed, realizing he was going to have to tell her if only to get to finish his dessert. ''Okay, fine. But it's nothing to worry about.'' He adjusted his weight on the couch, trying to get more comfortable as he stretched out his long legs under the table. The look of fear on her face made him sigh and he reached for her hand, linking his fingers through hers. ''Sophie, listen. Don't worry. I'm fine, really.''

"How many times and where were you shot?" she demanded, ignoring his comments about being fine. "Max, the last time I checked getting shot with a gun didn't qualify as being fine. Now spill it, all of it. How many times have you been shot, and where?"

"Three times," he admitted, watching her eyes go wide in horror. "But it's not that bad, Sophie, really," he insisted, giving her hand a squeeze. "It could have been a lot worse. And the doc would never have released me from the hospital if I wasn't fine."

"Never mind patronizing me, where were you shot?" she demanded, unwilling to let him charm his way out of this.

He sighed, realizing he was going to have to tell her whether he liked it or not. "One bullet bounced off my ribs, cracked three of them, but the doc said they'll be totally healed in about another month, I've just got to keep them taped and of course, try not to bump or jar them."

"Oh God," she moaned, staring at his chest. She couldn't see the tape because his shirt was covering it. "Where else?" She looked him over carefully, but couldn't see any evidence of any wounds. But Max had years of experience hiding his injuries, claiming it was just part of the job.

"One bullet caught me in the back of the calf." He grinned. "See, I'm not a complete idiot. The minute I realized I was caught in the crossfire, I tried to hustle my butt out of there. Hence the wound in the *back* of my calf." And the one that had hurt the worst, he wouldn't dare admit. "The doctor removed the bullet my first night in the hospital. Now there's just a big ugly scar." He shrugged. "No big deal."

"That's so comforting," she snapped sarcastically. "Okay, in the ribs and the calf, where else?"

He frowned. "Sophie, you're making too big a deal over this."

"Do you want another cannoli?" she asked through narrowed eyes, reaching for the platter and holding it in the air just out of his reach. "Or not?"

"You're a hardhearted woman, Sophie." He sighed, looking longingly at the platter of pastries. "Okay, the last shot grazed my collarbone." He shrugged, then winced at the pain that raced through his shoulder and down his arm. "My collarbone was fractured, but not too badly, so don't worry. It's a lot less painful now than when it first happened." He stretched his right arm out slowly and carefully, then flexed and wiggled his fingers, ignoring the pain that shot up his arm in an effort to prove he was fine. "See."

"Terrific. You've been shot three times, apparently been in the hospital for almost a month and this is the first I'm hearing about it," she fumed.

"I didn't want you to worry, Sophie."

"Good, I'll remember that the next time something happens around here and I don't tell you." Miffed, she shoved the platter of cannolis toward him, nearly spilling them off the edge in her annoyance.

"Sophie." Max set the platter down on the table and reached for her reluctant hand again. "It's not the same thing," he reasoned, causing her to scowl at him.

"Isn't it?" She turned to him, her temper simmering. "Max, do you realize how much the girls and I worry about you? I mean, don't you think it's time for you to start thinking about doing something a little less dangerous?"

She knew it was futile to even ask. Max lived and breathed his job, and had for as long as she'd known him. Asking him to give it up would be like asking Max to give up the very essence of who he was, something she could never even consider doing, in spite of the years of worry his career had caused.

"Actually, Sophie, I have been thinking about it," he admitted.

Shocked, she gaped at him. "You're kidding?"

He shook his head. "Nope. Actually, that's one of the reasons I came home. I figured I needed some time to heal, and maybe to think about some other options. So when I got home and got the girls' message, I thought this might be the perfect time to do both."

"I see," she said, not quite certain she should believe him. This did not sound like Max. Maybe he was hurt worse than he was letting on, she thought, letting her gaze go over him carefully again.

"Sophie, listen to me. I've done just about everything I set out to do. Accomplished all that anyone in my position can. I've got the awards, the prizes, the reputation and any plum assignment I've ever wanted. That's more than most men ever get to do professionally, so I just thought maybe this might be a good time to see what other options I've got on the table." He grinned. "You know there is more to life than a career."

"I never thought I'd ever hear you say you were thinking of giving up your career."

"Well, I don't know if I'd go so far as to say I'm giving it up. I'm thinking maybe I can just do some variation of what I do and that maybe there's room in my life for more than just work," Max said.

This was definitely *not* the Max she knew, Sophie thought. The Max she knew would be itching to get back to the front of whatever international spot was heating up. But this Max…well, she wasn't too sure of him and it made her nervous.

"Sounds like you've done some thinking about this already," she said carefully, wondering if there was more to this than he was letting on. Absently,

Sophie rubbed the back of her neck where the tingle had begun again.

"A little," he admitted slowly, turning to hold her gaze. "Actually, I've been doing a lot of thinking about a lot of things lately, Sophie. Things that maybe I've let go too long," he said thoughtfully, making Sophie frown.

"I see," she said, drawing her hand back from his to reach for her own coffee cup and wondering what to say next. She wasn't about to pry into his personal life, but clearly something was up with him. Max wasn't the kind of man to be introspective. With him, everything was always out in the open, but clearly there was something important on his mind. "So what do you think your options are?"

He smiled, reaching for his own coffee and taking a sip. "Well, my lawyer has been fielding offers for years from publishers interested in the story of my career."

"You're thinking of writing a book?" she asked, stunned and delighted.

"Thinking about it *only* right now," he cautioned. "I'm not certain I'm capable of even writing a whole book." He hated to admit the idea was both intimidating and daunting.

"Okay, but it's an option," Sophie said.

"Right. Then I can always teach," he added "I've had universities and colleges chasing me for years. But, it's not something I've ever considered just because I think teaching is what you do when you're done doing the real thing.''

''Thanks a lot, Max,'' she said in a huff, immediately defensive of her own profession.

He laughed, shaking his head. ''Sophie, I didn't mean that as an insult to you. You teach home economics because you not only love teaching, but you're a fabulous cook.''

''Exactly, but I couldn't teach it if I couldn't do it,'' she added defensively, leveling her chin in a way he found adorable.

''Sophie, whatever happened to your plans? I seem to recall that when we first met, you were seriously interested in owning your own little catering business,'' Max commented.

''You have a good memory,'' she said with a surprised smile, draining her coffee cup.

''So what happened?''

She chuckled, setting her cup down. ''Let's see. Marriage. Children. Responsibilities.'' She shrugged, trying not to let on how hard it had been to let her life's dream go for another dream. A family. She'd always thought she could have both, but it simply hadn't turned out that way.

''Life happened, I guess. When Michael and I were first married, I had to keep teaching simply because we needed the money. Then we found this big old house,'' she said with a happy sigh, glancing around her beloved home. ''And we both fell in love with it. But it was like a money pit because it needed so much work. Still needs so much work,'' she corrected with a grin.

"Lord, I remember what a mess it was," Max said with a rueful shake of his own head. "I have to admit I thought the two of you were nuts."

She laughed. "You and everyone else on the planet." Glancing around, Sophie leaned back against the couch, comfortably tucking her legs under her, realizing she was relaxed probably for the first time this evening.

Dating was very hard, nerve-wracking work, she realized, but with Max, she could just relax and be herself. It was nice.

"This house was everything I always thought a home should be, in spite of all the work." Memories of her early days with Michael surfaced, but those memories and that time was another lifetime ago. So much had happened since then. Mentally, Sophie pushed her memories away as she glanced around again. "I've still got a lot to do yet," she said with a wistful sigh. "But now if I've got the money, I don't have the time, and when I have the time, I don't seem to have the money." Shaking her head, she laughed, pulling down the afghan she'd hand-crocheted from the back of the couch and tucking it around her chilled legs. "I promised the girls more than two years ago I'd create a playroom for them in the basement. And I still haven't gotten to it."

"The basement?" Max said with a frown.

"Yeah. There's a full basement running under the entire length of the house. An attic upstairs as well. They're both a mess right now and little more than a depository for out-of-season clothes, toys and different holiday decorations. But the basement already has a half bath roughed in, so now all I have to do is find the time to clean the place out, and then go buy all the materials to finish it off."

"I'm not exactly a skilled carpenter, Sophie, but while I'm here, I'll be happy to take a stab at getting the basement cleaned out for you. Maybe even that attic."

"You will?" she said in surprise, making him laugh. "And is this before or after you recuperate?" She appreciated his offer, but realistically she had no idea how he'd accomplish anything with the extent of his injuries.

He laughed.

"Max, look, our home is your home, but that doesn't mean every time you come to visit I'm going to put you to work, or you have to work for your keep." She pressed her lips together. "Right now, I think it's vitally important that you just rest and recuperate."

"I will, but I don't want you thinking the only thing I know how to do is take pictures." He grinned at her. "And besides, the girls will help. It'll be a great project for us to do together."

"I guess it's just hard for me to believe you're actually going to be here long enough to get anything that involved done. You and I both know you get restless after being stranded in suburban bliss for a few weeks."

"Perhaps," he said thoughtfully. "But like I told you, I've got some time off and I plan on being here at least until Thanksgiving."

We'll see about that, she thought, but didn't say, knowing full well Max would be going stir-crazy after nearly a month.

"Well thanks, Max, I appreciate it, and I'm sure the girls would love to help in any project you come up with."

"I must admit in spite of the fact that I thought you and Michael were crazy when you bought this house, you've done wonders with this old place and really made it a home," Max said, glancing around the sprawling, cozily decorated living room and knowing how many hours of intensive labor and love she'd put into the place. "You've made it a home for everyone, Sophie," he said softly. "Including me, and I can't tell you how much I appreciate it."

Touched, she reached for his hand and gave it a squeeze. "Max, I told you when Michael and I got married you'd always have a home with us." She smiled. "The girls wouldn't have it any other way and neither would I. Besides, I appreciate how much time you spend with the girls while you're here.'' She turned to him, touched his stubbled cheek. ''They adore you, you know, and it's nice for them to have a positive male influence in their lives.''

''I know. And the feeling's mutual. I hope you know how much I love them and how much they mean to me.'' His brows drew together because he couldn't tell her all the things that were really in his heart for the girls.

Not wanting to dwell on his feelings, Max changed the subject.

''Now, you were telling me what happened to your dream of owning a catering business?'' he prompted.

She took a deep breath. ''Well, once we bought this house, we started trying to conceive. I couldn't quit working then because we needed my insurance. And then as the years passed, all the different doctors and specialists, the fertility tests, shots and the medicine, not to mention the in-vitro fertilization, which was only partially covered by my insurance was so expensive that there was no way I could quit working.''

''I know, Sophie, I remember,'' he said softly, knowing that was a particularly difficult time for her with Michael's drinking. A time he wasn't really aware of until after the fact. Knowing she'd basically gone through all of it alone because his brother

had been too selfish to support her made him wish
he'd been here for her.

"After the twins were finally born, I wanted to
stay home so I could be a full-time mother to them."
Her smile was tinged with sadness. "I wanted my
girls to have everything I never had." He nodded,
understanding completely. "And then Michael
died." Her voice had gone flat and he tightened his
grip on her hand. "I had no choice, I had to go back
to work to support us, but luckily my mother was
able to move in here so I could go back to work."

"How is your mother, by the way?" he asked
with an indulgent smile. He adored Carmella, Sophie's rather unconventional mother.

Sophie laughed. "As outrageous as usual. She's
taking tango lessons from Mr. Rizzo next door—"

"Is that what they're calling it these days?" Max
asked with a laugh and a lift of his brow.

"Yeah, well, she's really enjoying herself, and I
have to say it's nice to see her so happy."

Max was thoughtful for a moment. "Did it ever
occur to you what different paths you and your
mother chose after you lost your husbands?"

"Every day," she admitted with a sigh. "When
my father's plane disappeared, my mother simply
fell apart. She just couldn't handle anything simply
because my father had handled everything, and living on an Army base all those years, she never really
had to worry about doing much for herself. Every-

thing was right there. My dad's death just devastated her. But she grew up in a time when a woman's identity was completely dependent on her husband, so without my father, she was lost.

"Once my dad died, well, that started my mother's perpetual quest to find another man to give her an identity and to give her life meaning. I guess maybe that's why I never really resented her. I felt sorry for her because she never had the choices I had, or my girls will have. My mother didn't know how to do anything but be a wife, and even though that's hard for some people to understand, I do.'' Sophie laughed. "But at least now, thankfully, she's stopped marrying. But it took four or five bad marriages, not to mention numerous moves, to finally make her realize that she didn't have to marry a man to be happy or important.''

"Maybe that's why a home of your own and stability were so important to you,'' Max said, unable to resist reaching out and fingering the ends of her dark curls. They were, as he remembered, soft as silk.

"Absolutely,'' she confirmed. Knowing Max was touching her made her pulse jump erratically. "We moved so much when I was a kid that I knew I'd never want that for my own children.'' Her jaw set firmly. "One home, one place where they'd grow up and have lifelong, happy memories. That was and is still very important to me and why I fought so hard to hang on to this house.'' She looked at his face, shadowed by the now fading firelight, and something in his eyes made her heart ache. ''When Michael died, staying here, in this house, in the home we'd made for the girls was the most important thing to me and my mom knew it, so in order to keep the house I had to go back to work. I think in some ways coming here to live with us was my mom's way of saying how sorry she was about what happened after my dad died, and I guess she wanted to be certain I didn't go through what she had. Taking care of the girls has given my mom a renewed sense of purpose and importance that I don't think she's ever had before. I don't know what I would have done without her the past three years. Her presence has added just another measure of stability and security to the girls' lives.''

''I know, they adore her. As do I.'' Max frowned. ''So why didn't you start a catering business then? Your mom would have handled the girls.''

''I guess I could have,'' she began slowly, ''and in fact, it was my mother's love of cooking that got me so interested in it in the first place, but to tell you the truth, I didn't think it was wise to risk the little bit of capital I had saved for something as frivolous as a business. I needed a steady income to support all of us, not to mention health benefits, and teaching provided all of that for me as well as a wealth of stability.''

"Do you ever miss being home with the girls?" he asked, lifting a hand to brush a stray curl from her cheek. If ever there was a woman made for motherhood, it was Sophie. She was a natural and he couldn't help but admire how she'd successfully juggled so many balls in the air.

"Sometimes," she admitted a bit wistfully. "But because I work at the same school they attend, even though I'm in another building, I still get to see them during the day once in a while, and I'm right there in case there's an emergency. So I think that's helped ease the transition for all of us."

"Always the responsible one, aren't you, Sophie?" There was a hint of sadness in his voice because he knew that Sophie had given up so many of her own dreams in order to make a better life for everyone around her. She was a remarkable woman.

"I didn't really have a choice, Max." She glanced at him, and he could still see the pain Michael had inflicted on her. Even after all this time it hurt him to know his brother had been so unbearably cruel and insensitive to a woman who certainly didn't deserve it.

Sophie deserved nothing less than kindness, caring and unconditional love from her husband. Something he'd mistakenly believed his brother could and would give to her. He'd been so wrong. About so many things, he thought sadly.

"Someone had to be responsible," Sophie said,

reminding him of how irresponsible his own brother had become. To this day it still angered him.

"I know, Sophie, I know. But it wasn't fair, not to you or to anyone else."

"No one said life was fair, Max." She shrugged, then turned to him, surprised to find him watching her intently. "I've got my children, my mom, and a very stable life and to tell you the truth, that's all that matters to me. All that's ever mattered to me. As long as the girls are happy, I'm happy."

"I know, Sophie," he said carefully. "I know. But I guess that's another reason I've come home."

"What do you mean?" she asked.

He turned to look at her, studying those beautiful dark eyes that seemed to draw him like a magnet. "Because I think it's about time we finally talked about the girls."

Chapter Three

"What do you mean you want to talk about the girls?" Sophie asked cautiously, linking her fingers together in her lap to hide her sudden nervousness. Fear licked along every nerve ending at the enormous implications of his statement, implications she had no wish to get into. Now, or ever. They'd made an agreement never to speak about who the girls' biological father was and up until now, they'd both honored it—for the girls' sake. And she wasn't certain she wanted to risk breaking that agreement now.

"They're happy, healthy, doing well in school, so what on earth could you possibly want to talk about them for?" she forced herself to ask even as dread filled her.

"I'm worried about them."

She turned to him in surprise. "Worried? Why?"

"Well, Sophie, the idea of you dating has to be a new...experience for them."

She laughed in relief. So that's what this was about? Her dating. "Max, dating is a new experience for me, too." She looked at him. From the look on his face she wasn't certain if her dating was difficult for the girls.

Or for him.

Not for the first time did she feel a round of guilt over the fact that perhaps she was being disloyal to Michael and his memory. She had loved him once. Sophie swallowed the sudden lump in her throat. "It has been over three years, Max—"

"I know, I know," he said.

"I talked to the girls a lot over several weeks before I actually accepted and agreed to go out with James," Sophie said.

She felt like a sixteen-year-old explaining herself to her overprotective father. It was just a tad infuriating, and made worse by the fact that she didn't really want to be dating, not even James, in spite of how nice he was.

But everyone in her life kept telling her it was time to get on with her life, and so she thought it might be a good idea to go out once in a while, with a man, and socialize.

If she'd have known it was going to cause this many problems, she'd have never bothered.

"I even talked to my mother, Max," she explained. "My mom, the girls, everyone agreed they thought it might be a good idea for me to start socializing again."

"Yeah, well, socializing and dating are two different things, Sophie," he said with a decided scowl. "I approve of one."

"But not the other?" she asked with a lift of her brow. If he was deliberately trying to aggravate her, he was doing a very good job.

"It's just sort of sudden, don't you think?"

"You think my dating is *sudden?*" Shaking her head, Sophie looked at him, trying to figure out exactly what this was about. "Max, I've been alone three years, longer than that if you count the years before Michael's death when he was here in body, but not in any other way because of his drinking." Feeling a wave of sadness, Sophie glanced down at her linked fingers, not wanting to remember how quickly Michael and her marriage had gone down the drain. And how desperately she'd tried to save both her husband and her marriage. But she'd failed at both, she realized, and knew it would haunt her for a very long time. "Max, do you really want me to be alone the rest of my life?"

"You're not alone," Max pointed out. "You've got the girls, your mom. Me."

"You?" She glanced up at him in surprise, then chuckled. The last person in the world she would ever allow herself to lean on, need, or depend on was Max. She *knew* better.

"In the first place, Max, I see you maybe four or five times a year, and for only a few days at a time at that. And besides, I can't start depending on you—you've got your own life to lead."

"Do you hear me complaining?" he asked.

"That's not the point. I know you've tried very hard to be here for me and the girls, but you have your own life, your own career, and you know, one day you may want to get married. Then what?" she teased with a smile.

"Yeah, right," he all but sneered. "I'll be getting married right about the time pigs will be flying," he added with a scowl. There was only one woman in the world he'd ever considered marrying, and she was his brother's wife.

And she'd always been definitely off-limits.

Banishing the thoughts rolling around his mind, Max said, "I guess I'm just startled you didn't mention that you were going to start dating again. It really came as a surprise."

"You're surprised I didn't mention it to *you?*" Her temper was starting to simmer again. "I see," she said slowly. "Sort of like the way *you tell me* every time you begin dating someone new?"

"Come on, Sophie, don't be ridiculous, that's different."

"Different," she repeated. "And pray tell, Max, how is that different?"

"Well hell, Sophie, for one thing, I'm a single man—"

"A *man?*" Her voice edged upward in shock and anger. "You think because you're a man that makes it different? That's the most old-fashioned, macho, sexist thing I've ever heard you say," she fumed, wondering what on earth had gotten into him. Max may have been a lot of things, but *sexist* had never been one of them.

"I'm not only a man, Sophie, but I'm also *not* the mother of young twins."

"So what you're saying is that since I'm a mother, I'm apparently not supposed to have the needs and desires of a woman, right?"

"Yes." Max shook his head. "No. You're totally misinterpreting all of this, Sophie."

"I'm misinterpreting things?" Annoyed, she shook her head, sending her unruly black curls cascading around her head. "Uh, no, Max, I don't think so. From where I'm sitting, you just insulted me, denigrated my intelligence, and basically accused me of neglecting my children for my own selfish needs." She shook her head. "I'm sorry, Max, but I don't see it that way. I know that on some level you feel responsible for me, but quite frankly, I didn't think I needed to notify you or get your permission or approval before I started dating again—whether I'm a mother or not. I believe I'm totally capable of handling my own life and my own affairs, thank you very much.''

"Affairs," he thundered, his face going dark. ''Exactly what the hell is going on with you and James Beardsley? And why the hell didn't you just tell me you wanted to start dating again?''

''Why on earth would you even *expect* me to tell you that I was going to start dating again? And I hardly call waiting over three years sudden,'' she added tightly. ''And I might add, I didn't even know where in the world you were, but then again, I never do, now do I?''

''All right, point well taken,'' he admitted truthfully. ''But you and the girls always have my emergency cell phone number so you can reach me anytime, anywhere, and you know that.''

''And you think my dating again qualifies as an *emergency?*'' she demanded.

''That's not what I meant and you know it,'' he fumed.

''I see. Then would you please explain to me exactly what you meant? Because quite frankly, Max, right now you're digging a hole big enough to bury yourself in.''

He shrugged, realizing he was making a fool out

of himself and a mess out of this. "I guess I just never thought you would start dating again."

"Max," she began softly, laying a hand on his arm. A sudden thought struck her and she felt a hot sting of tears burn her eyes. "I know how close you and Michael were and how loyal you were to him. I didn't realize that my dating might make you feel as if I was being disloyal to Michael or his memory. I'm sorry if I've been insensitive, Max, I just never thought that you might have a problem with this."

"This has nothing to do with Michael," Max snapped. "This is about the girls."

"The girls?" One brow lifted and she looked at him carefully, really confused now. "And exactly *how* is this about the girls?"

"The girls aren't real partial to Beardsley, Sophie," he said, deciding he had no legs to stand on any more so he might just as well go with the truth.

She blinked at him. "Excuse me?"

"Beardsley," he repeated. "So tell me, Sophie, exactly what's going on between you and this guy?"

She sighed, then lifted her free hand to push her curls off her cheek. She felt more than a little embarrassed about discussing her personal life with Max. Which was ridiculous. She was a grown woman, perfectly capable of making decisions on her own, without anyone's approval or permission.

"Not that it's any of your business," she began. "But I don't think there's anything to tell yet. James is my boss and I've known him since I went back to work, right after Michael died.''

"So you've known the guy for about three years." Max needed to get a clearer picture of this relationship so he'd know how to deal with it. Or rather, *put an end* to it.

"Yeah," Sophie said with a nod. "I never really thought much about him, I mean more than professionally, until about six months ago."

"What happened six months ago?" Max asked with a scowl, reaching for the coffeepot and pouring himself a fresh cup.

"James started paying attention to me in a way that led me to believe his interest was a bit more than…professional." She flushed, embarrassed to have to reveal these details to Max. "Max, I'm really starting to lose my temper here. And unless you tell me what this is all about, I'm going to bed before you make me totally crazy."

"The girls don't like Beardsley," he said flatly, setting the coffeepot down with a thud. "And I can't say that I'm all that crazy about him, either."

"Max, how on earth can you say that?" she asked. "You've been here all of what…three hours? And you've concluded the girls don't like him and you don't either? Don't you think that's being just a bit unreasonable, not to mention unfair?"

"Unreasonable, hell, that guy yelled at Carrie, Sophie, and he scared her. That's more than I need to know about him.''

''Yelled at Carrie?'' Sophie shook her head, wondering if they were talking about the same little girls. ''Oh my goodness,'' she said with a laugh. ''Do you mean the day she hit James's car with her volleyball?''

''That would be the day.''

''Max. That was an accident, plain and simple, and James knew it. He didn't yell at Carrie, not really. But I can see how Carrie might have felt that way. James merely explained that his car was fairly new and he really didn't want her bouncing her ball against it,'' she clarified, realizing she was making excuses for James. In fact she'd been just as annoyed when he'd scolded Carrie that day as she was annoyed with Max right now. And she'd told James so. Loudly and clearly.

''And so you're telling me you're comfortable with a guy who cares more about his damn car than he does about your daughter's feelings?'' Max's deep voice rose in frustration.

''Of course not, that's ridiculous. But it seems to me, Max, that you're hardly in a position to criticize or really know what's going on with me or the girls since you haven't even seen us for almost three months.''

''You're right, Sophie. Absolutely right,'' he said. ''But I'm here now and that doesn't mean I'm just going to sit around and watch you marry James Beardsley.''

"Marry!" she cried in alarm. "Who the hell said anything about getting married?" Horrified at the mere thought of marriage to James, a man she barely knew, Sophie shook her head. "You're overreacting, Max, totally. I've had only a few official dates with the man, one date, I might add, that you did your best to ruin."

"Was I successful?" he asked with a grin, infuriating her even further.

"Yes, Max, if it makes you happy, you were successful," she snapped. "You totally ruined my date. Does that make you feel better?"

He tried to suppress his grin, but couldn't. "To tell you the truth, yeah, it does."

"Max, I don't know what this is about, but I think you're being ridiculous, not to mention a tad overprotective. And as for your remark about me getting married, as I said I haven't even thought of it, but if I had," she continued, holding up her hand when he opened his mouth, "if I had, I really can't see that it's any of your business."

"Anything that concerns the girls is my business."

She looked at him for a long moment, realizing they were now treading on very dangerous ground. Sophie could feel her nerves tighten and knew she wanted to get off this track of conversation.

"If I didn't know better, Max, I'd think you were jealous," she said quietly.

"Jealous?" he repeated in annoyance, his brows drawing together. It struck too close to home and he knew he'd have to change his tactics because he was in fact jealous. Jealous of the fact that Sophie might be interested in some other guy, and jealous over the fact that some other man might become a father to his girls. "I think my place in the girls' lives and hearts is safe, Sophie."

But he wasn't quite so certain about his place in *her* life and heart. And never had been because he'd deliberately stepped aside for his brother's sake and happiness. But doing it for his brother and for a stranger were two completely separate things.

Sophie glanced at him and her heart began to ache at the wounded look on his face. Why hadn't she realized Max might be threatened by another male in the girls' lives?

"Of course your place in the girls' hearts and lives is safe, Max," she said softly. "They adore you and you know it." She touched his cheek, wondering if this was the crux of Max's problem.

She and the girls were the only family Max had, and of course he'd feel threatened by the fact that another man might become important in their lives and worse, might take his place in their girls' lives and hearts.

"That will never change, Max, no matter who I date or marry."

"So then you *are* thinking of getting married again," he accused.

"Oh for Pete's sake," she fumed. "One date, one *failed* date, I might add, doesn't exactly lay the groundwork for marriage. As far as I know, James may never want to see me again considering my crazy family."

"Then he'd be an idiot," Max snapped.

"Max." Her voice held a warning, and he slouched lower on the couch, feeling miserable, physically and emotionally. This conversation hadn't gone exactly how he planned it.

"Sophie, I just want to make myself clear." He turned to her, and she could see the determination and something else in his eyes, something she couldn't read. "I'm giving you fair warning, I've got my eye on Beardsley. I don't like him, and I sure as hell don't like the idea of you getting involved with him or him being involved with the girls."

Sophie glared at him. "May I remind you once again I'm almost thirty years old, more than capable of choosing my own dates, let alone my own friends."

"You're absolutely right, Sophie," he all but snarled, surprising her. "You are old enough to choose the men you spend time with, but the girls aren't. They don't have a choice in the matter. Anyone you date will have a profound effect on the girls, and I think that's something you need to seriously think about before going out with just any guy who asks you.''

''Any guy who asks me!'' she snapped, giving her head an angry toss.

''Sophie,'' he said fiercely, holding his hand up to stop her so he could finish. ''If Beardsley ever, *ever* yells at the girls or scares them again, or does anything that so much as hurts their feelings, I swear I'm going to knock him right on his prim-and-proper backside. Got it?''

''Max!'' Horrified because she knew he meant it, Sophie glared at him. ''What on earth has gotten into you?'' She touched his forehead. ''Are you sure you weren't wounded in the head?''

''Don't be cute, Sophie, this isn't funny.''

''No, I agree with you, this isn't funny. Max, you don't have any idea what my life is like. You're not here day in and day out. You're not the one who is on duty twenty-four hours a day seven days a week. Do you have any idea how overwhelming it is to know I'm solely responsible for the care and raising of those precious little girls? Do you ever think about how daunting it is to know that one mistake and I could screw up their whole lives? Me, just me?''

"Come on, Sophie, don't you think you're being a bit dramatic?"

"Am I, Max?" she asked. "If you don't think one bad decision or one bad misjudgment can screw up people's lives think about the last decision Michael made. The one that told him he could get behind the wheel of a car when he was roaring drunk. That one mistake, Michael, that one bad decision has had serious consequences on all of our lives, so don't tell me I'm being too dramatic."

Her words hung in the air for a long moment, and Max suddenly felt like a jerk. She was right. He'd only been thinking of his own feelings, and not about hers, or what her life was like trying to raise the girls all on her own.

"I'm sorry, Sophie," Max said quietly. Both he and Sophie had suspected that Michael's accident that night hadn't really been an accident because he'd gotten drunk and then gotten behind the wheel during a horrendous winter storm, and he knew it still haunted her. "You're absolutely right." He shook his head. "I guess I never looked at things from your perspective."

"That's exactly my point, Max. You don't look at things that way because you don't have to. You're not a full-time parent, but I am. Raising the girls alone is not something I'd ever thought about doing—"

"It wasn't something any of us considered, Sophie,'' he added with a frown. ''None of us ever even considered it.''

''I know, Max,'' she said quietly, ''and quite frankly, it's very daunting. And I'm not ashamed to admit it's also very lonely at times,'' she added. ''I've been alone a lot longer than the three years Michael has been gone, and you know it. I've been a single parent to the girls almost from the moment they were born and you, better than anyone, know it.''

No one would ever know or understand the extreme loneliness that had plagued her from the moment she'd learned she was pregnant. It was at that precise moment, when they learned their dream of having a family was going to come true, that Michael had changed, totaling withdrawing from her, leaving her pregnant and alone to fend for herself.

During the ensuing years, he became cold, morose and resentful. He became a man she no longer knew. Or loved. But she feared leaving him in the emotional state he was in.

''Once in a while it might be nice to have someone to turn to for help and support and just to share things with, the big things and the little things,'' she finished.

''Sophie, I'm sorry. I haven't handled any of this very well. But I guess I was just caught off guard to find out you were seeing someone.''

''Max.'' She squeezed his hand, wishing she

could keep him there, right next to her and safe forever. "I understand. Truly," she said, forcing a smile. "I can see how this might have come as a shock to you, and I guess I just didn't think you'd care."

"Sophie." His beautiful blue eyes glittered and he stroked a finger down her cheek. "I care about *anything* that involves you. Or the girls," he added, fearful of letting her know what was really in his heart, especially now that she was apparently seeing someone else.

It hurt, he realized, and a helluva lot more than just his pride.

"I guess I never thought about you being lonely," he admitted with a sheepish grin.

"You can be surrounded by a crowd, Max, and still be lonely," she said softly, lifting her gaze to his.

"I know," he responded just as quietly, getting snagged by that beautiful dark gaze of hers. He'd always thought she'd had the most beautiful, mesmerizing eyes in the world. They seemed to drag him in like a whirlpool, then simply wouldn't let him go.

When she swiped at her eyes and sniffled again, he swore, then pulled her to him in a hug, wrapping his arms around her in the same way he'd wrapped his arms around Carrie earlier. "Okay, so I've behaved like a jerk." He shrugged, glancing down at her. "It's probably not the first time, and definitely won't be the last." Her dark, shiny hair smelled like wildflowers. The scent had always driven him crazy. "If I'd have known you wanted to start socializing and dating, well, hell, I'd have asked you out myself."

Her head came up so fast she almost conked him on the chin. "You?" She blinked at him, then chuckled to hide her nervousness at his words. "Why on earth would you ask me out?"

He drew back, slightly offended. "Well, why on earth wouldn't I?"

"Well, let's see, Max. To start with you're my brother-in-law—"

"So what?" He was sick and tired of only having her see him as Michael's big brother. When on earth was she going to start seeing him as a man? His own man, a totally separate entity from Michael. "I was a man a helluva long time before I became your brother-in-law."

"That's true," she said. "But you just got through saying you'd get married when pigs would fly. So what on earth would be the point of you asking me out?"

"Well, the point is that you'd be able to start socializing and dating, and with someone you know better than anyone else in the world. Someone you know has your best interests at heart, and who already loves your daughters. And may I remind you,

you also said *you* never wanted to get married again, but you're dating Beardsley, aren't you? So exactly what's the difference? Just because someone doesn't want to get married doesn't mean they have to be alone for the rest of their life, as someone very intelligent just pointed out to me," he reminded her with a grin.

"That's true," she had to admit. "But why on earth would you want to date *me?*" Shaking her head, she laughed. "I mean, Max, you probably know me better than even Michael did." Which was true. She and Max had always been able to talk for hours and hours about everything and nothing.

Yet, she and Michael, after those first couple of years, when they'd first started having trouble conceiving, hadn't been able to talk or share anything.

Michael had become withdrawn and morose, blaming first her, then himself for their infertility. Their relationship had become more and more strained as the years passed and they were unable to conceive until it was as if they were two strangers simply occupying the same house. It had been a horrible time in her life, a time when she'd never felt quite so lonely or all alone.

"Think of how comfortable that makes things," Max said. "No unpleasant surprises."

He had a point, she had to acknowledge, but it just seemed so odd. For so long she'd tried to keep her feelings for Max under control. How on earth would she ever be able to do that if she were dating him, knowing he'd be leaving in a month or so.

"Max, let's be sensible," she said, trying to protect her heart and her emotions. She wasn't sure she'd be able to control either if she were actually in a romantic situation with him, and she was pretty sure dating qualified as a romantic situation.

"Why?" he asked. "I happen to think I'm being very sensible, Sophie. I mean think about it. If this whole dating thing is because you're lonely, and want someone to spend time with, someone you can have fun with, and yet not worry about it getting serious, I would think I'd be the perfect person." He was grasping at straws here, and he knew it. But if she could date Beardsley, then she sure as hell could date him. He'd waited years for the opportunity, years for Sophie to first get over her grief, and then get accustomed to thinking of him as something other than her protective brother-in-law. If he didn't do something drastic and soon, he was never going to get a chance to show her what they could have together. Or how he really felt about her. Or that he could be the kind of man she wanted and needed, in spite of his past and his career.

"And then of course I have the added advantage of knowing your kids love and approve of me, as opposed to Beardsley who they neither like nor approve of," he reminded her, bringing on another round of guilt.

"Max." She lifted her head, and met his gaze, surprised by the intensity in his eyes. "Let's face it, everything you've said is true and quite logical. But I'm not at all like the women you normally date. I mean, I'm a single mother, I'm almost thirty, I don't have a dazzling life, well-heeled friends, or designer clothes."

"That's precisely the point, Sophie. You're not at all like any other woman, and I'm not like any other man," he said. "But we're already friends. We have a special bond between us," he added quietly. "And we know each other better than anyone else, we have shared and mutual interests—the girls. Not to mention the fact that we get along so well it would seem just natural."

"You really think so?" she asked hesitantly, her heart and mind torn. Her heart wanted to just say yes, to just agree to date Max, but her mind was flashing yellow caution signs everywhere she looked.

"I know so." He tightened his arms around her. "So how about it? Would you like to go out tomorrow night?"

"Tomorrow night?" she stammered, feeling more nervous at the moment than she'd felt when she first agreed to go out with James. Good Lord, James. What on earth was she going to tell him? Well, she had told him their dating was merely a trial situation.

"Yeah, tomorrow. It's Saturday, a traditional date night."

"But it's supposed to be pizza and movie night with the girls."

"So, I'm sure your mom wouldn't mind baby-sitting. She can even invite Mr. Rizzo next door. I'm sure the girls would love that."

"You think so?" she asked, realizing that her heart was getting very close to overruling her cautious mind.

"I know so." He nuzzled her neck, savoring and inhaling her wonderful scent. "So what do you say? Is it a deal?"

"Max, before I say yes, what happens when you leave? And you will, you know. We both know it," she added, already hurting at the thought.

"Sophie, for right now, let's just take things one day at a time, okay?" he asked with a frown, knowing he wasn't quite so sure he was leaving this time as she was, but it was still far too early to be telling Sophie that.

He wasn't going to say anything to anyone until he'd had some time to recuperate, rest, and feel the entire situation with her and the girls out.

"Do you think you can handle that, Sophie? One day at a time. Let's handle only today's problems today. We can worry about tomorrow tomorrow. So, is it a date?"

Sophie sighed, wondering if she'd lost her mind.

"It's a date, Max. Tomorrow night. But," she cautioned, lifting a finger in the air in warning, "that's provided my mom can stay with the girls."

"I'll ask her personally," he assured her, grabbing her finger and kissing it gently. "This will be fun," he said, kissing her forehead, then letting his lips slide down across her eyes, her cheeks, finally ending at the corner of her mouth where he gently nibbled.

"Max." His name came out half plea, half prayer and Sophie let her eyes close on the pleasure of his mouth, clutching his shirt tighter. His lips continued to nibble, then slowly moved over hers. Unconsciously, she leaned into him, pressing against his hardness.

"Nothing wrong with sealing our deal with a kiss," he murmured.

A log in the fireplace shifted, then plopped to the bottom, creating a shower of firelight, but it was nothing compared to the heat and fire building inside of her.

She moaned softly when Max's lips slid over hers, capturing and mesmerizing her. Her heart did a quick, wild tumble, then continued its rapid pace, making her fear it would simply tumble out of place as she slid her arms up his chest—remembering his injured ribs at the last minute—to anchor around his neck.

Max's breath sighed out of him as her scent infiltrated his every sense, making him both giddy and dizzy. As he tightened his arms around her, his hands itched to peel the material away from her body, to see and revel in all her beauty.

Kissing Sophie had to be one of God's greatest pleasures, he decided, as he took the kiss deeper, held her tighter.

She made soft, female sounds deep in her throat, sounds of need, of desire, sounds that made his blood surge madly, as urges as old and primitive as time began to move through him with a force and heat he knew he wouldn't be able to control.

With a sigh, Max knew he had to rein himself in. *Now.* He drew back reluctantly, seeing her lids flutter open, wide and dreamy.

"Sophie." It was all he could manage, her name. Unable to resist, he pressed his mouth to hers again, unwilling to break contact, wanting more of the sweetness of her.

"Max." Shocked by her own response, Sophie pressed her hand to his chest, fearing if she didn't put some barrier between them, she'd go right back into his arms again.

And that would be far too dangerous a move on her part, she reminded herself. Dating him was one thing. But she was supposed to be keeping her distance, both physically and emotionally. She wasn't supposed to allow Max to sneak past her defenses. But he had. And she hadn't a clue what to do about it since she seemed almost powerless to stop him once he touched her.

One touch and she was like putty in his hands. So much for willpower.

"I... I think we'd better call it a night." Her voice was shakier than she would have liked, but it was hard to speak when her entire system had gone haywire.

"Good idea." Max stretched, then stifled a yawn, glancing at the fire. "I'm glad I'm home, Sophie," he said quietly, turning to her.

Carefully, as if it required intense concentration, she began to fold up the afghan she'd had around her knees, before glancing up at him with a smile. "I am, too, Max. I am, too."

Max stood, then held out his hand to her. For a second, she simply stared at it, fearful about touching him again. Then, realizing she was being ridiculous, she took his hand and allowed him to help her to her feet.

"I'll help clean up the rest of this mess in the morning," he said, glancing at the coffeepot, the empty cups and dessert plates.

"Don't worry about it, Max. It's no big deal." She laid the afghan over the couch. "The girls have ballet class first thing in the morning, so if we're gone when you get up, don't worry about it."

Stifling another yawn and rubbing his aching shoulder, Max nodded in acknowledgment. "I have

a feeling I won't be worrying about anything tomorrow. I'm beat. Guest room in the same place?''
he asked. She nodded.

''Fourth door on the right. There's fresh linens on
the bed and clean towels in the bath.''

''Sounds like you were expecting me?'' he said
with a smile, dropping his arm around her shoulder
and leading them toward the steps.

''I never know when or who will be bunking
over,'' she said, slipping her arm around his waist.
There was an intimacy about walking to the stairs
with their arms around each other, Sophie thought.
An intimacy that only came after living with someone for a long time and knowing them well. It was
an intimacy she'd never had with Michael, even
though they'd been married almost seven years.

''You sure you're okay about tonight, Sophie?''
Max asked as he led her up the stairs.

''Yes, I'm okay, Max.'' She stopped at the top of
the stairs, grateful there was only a night-light casting shadows. Otherwise he'd realize she was lying.

She'd agreed to date him and she'd honor her
promise.

But she had a feeling this dating thing was merely
a ploy to get her to stop seeing James, since Max
clearly didn't like or trust the man.

And right now, for whatever reason, Max thought
he wanted to date her, but the reality of it was two
little girls and a very boring single mom couldn't

hope to duplicate or replace the kind of wild adventures or experiences his real life had to offer.

No matter how much Sophie wished it or wanted it.

In a month or so, Max would be gone again, and she could only hope this time he wouldn't leave her and her daughters with broken hearts.

Chapter Four

"Mama, you're pouring coffee in my cereal," Mary complained, frowning up at her mother.

"What?" Sophie glanced down at the slightly panicked sound in her daughter's voice. "Oh. Oh. Sweetheart, I'm so sorry." Grabbing her daughter's bowl of cereal and now coffee, she quickly moved to the sink and dumped Mary's cereal out. "I'm so sorry, honey," Sophie said as she set the coffeepot down and grabbed a clean bowl from the cabinet. "Mama's a bit tired this morning." And that, she thought, was a mild understatement.

She'd barely slept last night, and when she did, she'd had wicked, vivid dreams about Max, dreams that left her exhausted and frustrated, not to mention annoyed at herself for being so ridiculous.

Long ago, when she'd first met Michael and Max she'd realized that Max, with his restlessness and high-flying lifestyle was not the man for her. Nothing had changed in the ensuing years, so it was ridiculous for her to harbor fantasies about a man who was so clearly wrong for her and her little family.

"Mama, are you okay?" Carrie asked, her gaze going from her sister to her mother, then back again.

"Okay?" Sophie glanced at Carrie, then blinked, realizing she'd been daydreaming again. "Why, honey? Did I pour coffee in your cereal, too?"

"No, Mama, you didn't give me any cereal yet," Carrie complained. "And if we don't hurry up we're gonna be late for our ballet class. And you know Miss Fontaine fines us if we're late."

Nodding, Sophie glanced at the clock, cursed softly, then hurried to get another bowl from the cupboard. She had to get her act together this morning, she thought as she poured cereal for Carrie.

Sunlight streamed through the bay window in the sprawling farmhouse kitchen, smothering everything in a warm, golden morning glow. Remodeled when she and Michael had first bought the house almost ten years ago, the kitchen floors were now gorgeous, golden oak planks, while the counters were a deep blue geometric patterned ceramic. All the appliances were state-of-the-art stainless steel and built in, while the kitchen table, a very old oak parson's table that sprawled nearly the entire length of the kitchen had been lovingly hand-refinished by Sophie herself. Eight chairs in a matching hue of oak were tucked all around the table, leaving more than enough room to move about in the spacious room.

Sophie sighed as she slid the box of cereal back into the cabinet. Even though it was Saturday, and there was no school, there were still plenty of chores to be done. First the girls had to be shuttled to ballet class, then she'd drop them off back home for her mother to watch while she went grocery shopping, to the bank, the dry cleaners and the pharmacy to refill Carrie's allergy medicine. All of this was before she went to the video store to rent movies for the girls' Saturday night pizza and movie night.

Then she still had to come home, unload everything, then prepare her pizza dough for dinner, plan her meals for the next week, and of course, do laundry. Some day off, she mused.

The double café doors swung open and Max grunted softly when he saw the three of them. ''Morning,'' he mumbled, rubbing the top of his black head.

He was barefoot, had pulled on a scruffy, wrinkled pair of jeans that were zipped, but not buttoned, and wore an old, faded sleeveless college T-shirt that molded like warm wax to his finely chiseled body. There was a faint line of bruises running down his right shoulder, no doubt from his recent injuries.

"Morning, Uncle Max," the girls caroled in unison.

"Coffee," he muttered, taking the large, empty mug Sophie offered him with a nod of thanks. He filled his cup to the brim, then closed his eyes and took a long sip, sighing in pleasure as the caffeine jolted his system into something near normalcy.

"So where are you two off to so early in the morning and dressed so pretty?" he asked the girls, grabbing a chair and sitting down next to Mary.

"Ballet class," she said with a grin as she shoveled cereal into her mouth. She glanced down at her pink leotard and pink tights and ballet shoes. "Carrie and I take ballet class every Saturday."

"And we're doing good, too," Carrie said around a mouthful of cereal. "Aren't we, Mama?"

"Absolutely," Sophie said with a smile as she finished the last of her coffee and poured herself another fortifying cup.

"And we're gonna be in a recital," Mary added. "A ballet recital..." Her voice trailed off and she scratched her head. "But I don't remember when."

Sophie smiled, smoothing a hand over her daughter's hair. "It's the week of Thanksgiving, sweetheart, remember?"

"Oh yeah," Mary said with a shrug and a nod before resuming spooning cereal into her mouth.

Max nodded. "That's right, your mother told me about your classes." He glanced up at Sophie. "So what's on the agenda after the girls finish ballet class?"

"After ballet, I'll bring the girls back here and my mom will watch them while I finish my Saturday errands."

"What time does ballet class let out?"

Sophie glanced at her watch. "About ten-thirty. Why?" she asked.

"If you give me the address, I'll pick them up." He flashed a wink at the girls. "We have some errands of our own to run this morning. That way once you drop them off, you can get started on your errands without having to wait for the girls to finish their class." Max sipped his coffee, watching Sophie over the rim.

She hadn't slept well, he noted, if the shadows under her eyes were any indication. He had a feeling he'd totally thrown her for a loop last night, but then, that *had* been his intention.

It wasn't often he was able to catch a woman like Sophie off her guard, and he wasn't about to look a gift horse in the mouth. While she thought they were merely "dating," he fully intended to take advantage of the time he had to woo and win her.

"Okay," Sophie said cautiously, realizing that it would save her at least an hour, and an hour on a day when she was so busy could be a lifesaver.

"That will work out fine." She reached for her purse on the counter, and dug for a pen and a piece of paper to write the address of the dance studio on it for Max.

Max grinned. "Here comes your mother."

"How can you tell?" Sophie asked with a frown, handing him the slip of paper.

"I can smell her perfume," Max said with another grin, getting up to refill his empty coffee mug. "I can always smell your mother's trademark perfume."

The double swinging café door opened and Carmella Maria Rogatti swept into the room with the aura and elegance of a queen greeting her court, a wide, welcoming smile on her red-tinted lips.

"Maximillian, darling, how wonderful to see you." Carm laughed, patting her perfectly coiffed head as she posed in the doorway, letting the swinging doors close behind her. "I thought I sensed a gorgeous man," she added with a grin, walking straight into Max's open arms.

"How are you, sweetheart?" Max asked, planting a loud, smacking kiss on Carm's cheek as he swung her around in a hug. "You look fabulous, as usual."

At sixty-three, Carmella accentuated her petite frame by wearing only dark, slimming colors, and enormous, pencil-thin high heels that would give a younger, less courageous woman a nosebleed.

Her short black hair, now artfully streaked with

silver, emphasized her gold-dusted skin and accentuated her dark eyes.

"I *am* absolutely spectacular, Max," she admitted to Max as he set her back down on her high-heeled feet, then drew back to look at him. "I'd ask how you are, but I can see for myself," she said, casting a critical eye toward him. "You're malnourished, weary and tired." She pulled at his T-shirt. "Not to mention you could stand to put on a few pounds."

Max shook his head. "Ahh, Carm, sounds to me like that's your intro into 'it's time for you to get married and have someone look after you' speech."

"It's so tedious to be predictable," Carm said with a sigh and a wave of her perfectly manicured hands. "But it's well past time for you to marry and settle down if you ask me."

"Mom," Sophie said in a cautious tone, trying to smother a smile. If her mother had her way, everyone in the world would be married. Repeatedly and often. "Don't nag."

"Nag, dear?" Her mother drew back and theatrically placed her hand on her heart. "Me? What an utterly ridiculous idea. I'd never dream of nagging Max, now would I, dear?" she asked, turning to him and batting innocent eyes.

"Nope, not you, Carm. But you do look spectacular." He grinned. "Now why do I have a feeling Mr. Rizzo next door has something to do with that sparkle in your eyes?'' Max teased, making her flush a bit and fan her face with her hand.

"Rino Rizzo is a lovely man, dear, but the sparkle in my eyes is because I'm so delighted to see you. It's been far too long.'' Affectionately, she reached up and squeezed his cheeks between her hands. "Girls, have you ever seen a more gorgeous man in your life?''

"No, Grandma,'' the girls giggled, knowing their lines perfectly. Carm and Max did this every time he came home.

Carm turned back to Max. "You're lucky I'm not twenty—''

"Ten, Carm,'' he corrected. "Only ten years.''

"Very well,'' she agreed cheerfully. "You're lucky I'm not ten years younger or I'd give you a run for your money, young man.''

"And you're lucky I'm not ten years older or I'd take you up on your offer and send Rino Rizzo packing.''

Carm patted his cheek and sighed. "It's such a pity youth is wasted on the young.'' Still smiling, she glanced at her daughter. "And how are you this morning, my beautiful daughter?'' she asked, as she bent to kiss each of her granddaughter's shiny dark heads, before grabbing a mug from the mug tree on the counter to pour her own coffee.

"I'm fine, Mom.'' Sophie glanced at her watch

again. "But if we don't get going we're going to be late."

"Ballet class?"

"Yes, Mom." Deliberately, Sophie glanced at Max. He met her gaze with a confused look, then remembered he was supposed to arrange their sitter for this evening.

"Uh... Carm, do you have any plans tonight?"

She looked at Max with a saucy grin. "For you, I'll cancel them." Batting her lashes at him to make her granddaughters giggle, Carm patted her hair again. "Exactly what did you have in mind, darling?"

Max realized he was nervous, and tried to shake the sensation away. He wasn't a man who got nervous. With his job that was a good way to get dead—fast. He didn't mind dodging bullets in a foreign land, but somehow actually going on a date with Sophie made him nervous. "Well, uh. Sophie and I are going out tonight, on a date," he clarified, glancing up to see Carm and the girls staring at him in wide-eyed surprise. "And uh...we...we were wondering if you'd be able to sit with the girls."

"I know it's pizza and movie night, girls," Sophie injected nervously, "but I'll still pick up some movies on my way home from grocery shopping. Since I probably won't be home in time to make your pizza, girls, you can order one. Mom, if you've got something else planned, I'm sure—"

"Don't be ridiculous," Carm said with a wave of her hand. "I'd love to spend the evening with my darling granddaughters. We can have an old-fashioned girls' night complete with pizza and ice-cream sodas. What do you think of that, girls?"

Carrie and Mary's faces lit up like a Christmas tree and Carm laughed in pure joy at making her granddaughters so happy.

"Can we have popcorn, Grandma?"

"Buckets of it," Carm confirmed with a nod.

"Ice cream?"

"Barrels of that as well," Carm said. "And then, when the popcorn and ice cream are gone, we'll rummage around for some candy." She winked at her granddaughters. "I know your mother has some Halloween candy hidden somewhere around here," she said, pointing her finger toward the cabinet over the refrigerator where Sophie always hid the Halloween candy. "We can set up a treasure hunt to find it," she whispered, still pointing at the cabinet where the candy was hidden.

"You can invite Mr. Rizzo if you want," Max added. "We don't want to screw up your plans for the evening."

"Darling, that's very thoughtful of you, but actually, Rino's gone to visit his daughter for the weekend, so this will work out splendidly. Absolutely splendidly. The girls and I haven't had an evening to ourselves in ages." She sipped her coffee.

"What do you think, girls? Manicures? Pedicures? Facials? All topped off by one of Gram's soon-to-be-famous delicious bubble baths?"

"Yippee," the girls caroled, all but bouncing out of their chairs in excitement and clapping their hands together.

"While you're at ballet class, I'll run out and get some fabulous snacks and munchies for tonight, as well as some vibrant new nail polish and some lovely lavender-scented bubble bath I've had my eye on," Carm said, tapping her nail against her lip in thought. "And maybe we can even convince your mom to let us use some of that new wash-in hair dye, what do you think, girls?"

"Can I have pink?" Mary asked wide-eyed and grinning.

"Absolutely, darling. Pink has always been your color anyway," Carm said, turning to Carrie. "And you darling, what color would you like your hair to be?" she asked softly, always mindful that Carrie didn't have the brazen confidence of Mary.

Blinking shyly, Carrie slid off her chair to whisper in her grandmother's ear. Carm gave her a quick hug and a smile. "Why that's a fabulous, idea, Carrie, just fabulous." She tilted Carrie's dark head to and fro. "Yes, dear, I think purple with yellow dots will be splendid, absolutely splendid." She kissed Carrie's nose. "And they're your colors, too, dear."

"Mom," Sophie began in caution. "The girls have to go to school on Monday."

"I know, dreadful isn't it?" Carm said with a wink. "But it's a temporary hair dye, dear, washes out with shampoo, so never fear. I won't do any permanent damage."

"And Mom, remember, no blue, purple or black nail polish. It's not allowed at school."

"Such spoilsports," her mother said with a frown. "Honestly." Carm brightened suddenly. "Well, it *is* almost Halloween. The big Halloween festival is next weekend so I think maybe we might actually go with orange nail polish." She tapped a red-tinted nail to her lip again. "A bright orange." Her delicate brows drew together. "Are you sure about the black, darling?" she asked, turning to her daughter. "We could do some wonderful creative nail designs with it." Carm beamed at her granddaughters. "Maybe the girls could even enter their nails in one of the contests at the festival?"

"No black," Sophie said again, as she drained her coffee cup and set it in the sink. She could just see James's face if her daughters showed up at school with purple hair and black nail polish. Sophie rolled her eyes. She didn't even want to think of the lecture she'd get or the fallout.

"We've got to get going." Sophie grabbed her purse off the counter. "Come on, girls, I'll pull the car out." She turned to Max. "And you'll pick them up from ballet class at ten-thirty?'' she asked worriedly.

''On the dot.'' He held up the paper with the address on it. ''Scout's honor.''

Carrie and Mary slid from their chairs to kiss their grandmother and their uncle.

''Are you really going on a date with Mama tonight?'' Mary whispered.

''Yep, I am really going on a date with your mother,'' he confirmed with a grin, giving her a thumbs up signal.

''And it's about damn time, too,'' Carm said with a smile as the girls raced out of the room to join their mother. ''It's about damn time, Maximillian.'' She lifted her mug in the air in salute. ''I was beginning to worry about you, Max, but you've restored my faith in the male species.'' She laughed suddenly. ''Not an easy feat considering my rather illustrious history.''

''So where do we have to go next, Uncle Max?'' Mary asked, as she bit into her fast-food hamburger and squirmed on the bench seat of the restaurant. The Saturday-afternoon lunch crowd was comprised of harassed mothers and noisy, hungry toddlers.

Max reached into the back pocket of his jeans and pulled out the list he'd made. ''Well, we've been to the florist, and the building supply—''

''Uncle Max, what'cha gonna do with all those

boards you bought?'' Carrie asked, putting a French fry in her mouth.

''We're going to build you girls a playroom.''

Carrie's eyes rounded. ''Really?'' she said in awe.

''Really.'' Max popped the last of his burger in his mouth and checked the time on his watch. ''But first, we have to thoroughly clean out the basement.'' Max looked at the girls steadily. ''Do you think you girls are up to that?''

Carrie and Mary exchanged glances. ''Yep, Uncle Max,'' Mary said, speaking for the both of them.

''Yeah, Uncle Max, we want to help,'' Carrie added.

''It's probably going to take several weeks of hard work after school,'' he cautioned.

''We don't mind, Uncle Max, we're good workers,'' Carrie added.

''Yeah, Uncle Max, even Grandma says we work hard.''

''Good.'' Still studying his list, Max absently kissed them both on the head. A thought had been percolating in his mind all day, actually all night, ever since he and Sophie had talked last night, but he needed to clear it with the girls.

''Girls, does your mother ever use the extra garage that's at the back of the house?''

''You mean that old building that used to be for

horses and buggies or something?'' Mary asked, frowning.

''Yeah, the one we're not ever s'pose to go inside of,'' Carrie added.

''That's the one,'' Max said with a nod. The carriage house had originally been built when horse and buggies were the rage. As a result, in addition to the modern two-car garage that had been built at the back end of the property by previous owners, there was also an unused second building, sort of an old-fashioned carriage house. He knew Michael had once talked about turning it into a workshop, but had never gotten around to doing anything about it, and so now it sat, empty, paint peeling, and all but falling down around itself.

Last night, lying in bed, unable to sleep, he'd gotten up and stared out his window, thinking. And that's when he saw the building, and the idea hit him.

''Nah, we don't use it for nuthin','' Mary said, shoving several fries in her mouth and talking around them. ''Mama says it's a nuisance.''

''A nuisance, huh?'' Max said with a grin, taking a sip of his soft drink.

''Uncle Max,'' Carrie began slowly, derailing his thoughts. ''Me and Carrie, could we…uh…ask you something?''

Max glanced up, his gaze going from one little girl to the other. Realizing this was important to them, he stuffed his list back in his pocket, and gave them his full attention.

"Sure, sweetheart," he said, drawing her into the circle of his arms. "What's on your mind?"

Grinning, Carrie glanced at her sister. She hesitated a moment, shoving her hair out of her face as she took a deep breath, then blew it out, trying to gather her courage. "Next weekend is Halloween, and…uh…we was wondering if you'd maybe take us to the big Halloween festival?"

"Yeah, Uncle Max," Mary rushed on. "See, it's at nighttime, on Friday, and usually Mama's too tired from working all day, so we haven't gone in a while. We'll do all our chores, and eat all our dinner, but we really, really, really want to go. Please, Uncle Max. Pul-lease?"

"Uh, and Uncle Max," Carrie said, exchanging a glance with Mary that said more than words. "Mr. Bugs-bee offered to take Mama to the festival on Friday cuz it's at the school and he's in charge of it, but we don't want to go with him." With her lower lip trembling in an almost-pout, Carrie grabbed his hand and squeezed. "So could we please go with you? Please?"

"Yeah, Uncle Max. We don't want to go anywhere with the bug-man," Mary said defiantly, crossing her arms across her chest. "We'd rather stay home," she said with a nod of her head that mimicked her sister's.

Max shook his head, sitting back down on the bench and drawing both girls into his arms. He'd deal with Sophie going out with Beardsley on Friday, later. Right now he had to reassure the girls.

"First of all, I'll take you guys anywhere you want to go as long as it's all right with your mother. And second, you don't have to go *anywhere* with Mr. Beardsley if you don't want to, not ever again, you got it?" Looking at Carrie's troubled face and eyes, he realized she was scared again, and he swore under his breath. Little kids shouldn't have to be afraid or worried about anything.

Especially *his* kids, he thought, furiously.

"Uncle Max, did you say a bad word?" Eyes wide, Carrie covered her mouth with her hand to hide a giggle.

"I did," he admitted, looking sheepish, realizing the girls had unbelievable hearing so he'd better watch his tongue. "I'm sorry, honey, it's just that Mr. Beardsley makes me crazy."

"He makes us crazy, too, Uncle Max." Mary elbowed her sister. "But we won't tell Mama you said a bad word."

"Mama doesn't like bad words," Carrie confirmed.

"Thanks, sweetheart." Max was thoughtful for a moment. "Girls, listen to me very carefully. If Mr. Beardsley wants to take you somewhere, or do something with you girls that you don't want to do, just tell him 'thank you very much, Mr. Beardsley, but our Uncle Max is going to take us.'"

Carrie's eyes widened into saucers. "But what if he gets mad at us, Uncle Max?" she whispered, fear shimmering off her. "He doesn't like me, remember."

His protectiveness toward the girls knew no bounds, and if Beardsley didn't quit scaring them, they were definitely going to have words. Strong words. He'd just about had his full of this guy. And knew, after talking to Sophie last night that Beardsley probably had poor Sophie buffaloed.

But why hadn't he expected it?

Sophie had very little experience with men, other than with him and Michael. She wasn't a dater, and never had been, not even when she was younger. Sophie had always been very sweet, but very serious about life and what she'd wanted out of it.

So how on earth could he expect her to see what a knucklehead Beardsley really was? Or the fact that he was showing Sophie only what he wanted her to see, and not who or what he really was?

Maybe, just maybe it was time to show Sophie who the real Beardsley was, Max thought. But he'd have to be careful not to do anything to upset the girls, or worse, tick Sophie off.

No, he decided, he'd probably have to let Beardsley show his true colors on his own, but that didn't mean he wasn't going to keep an eye on the guy. A careful eye.

"Girls, you never, ever have to worry or fear anyone as long as Uncle Max is alive, you got it?" he asked, tilting first Mary, then Carrie's chins up so he could meet their gazes. "Do you understand?"

"We understand, Uncle Max," Mary said, as she threw her arms around him.

"And we love you, Uncle Max," Carrie added with a sniffle.

"And I love you both. Tons and tons. But I don't want you worrying anymore about Mr. Beardsley. I promise you Uncle Max is going to take care of him. If all goes well, you may have actually seen the last of him dating your mother."

It was almost four-thirty by the time Sophie finally got home for the day. Exhausted from running around all day, and cranky from fighting crowds everywhere she went, she was famished, had a roaring headache, and wanted only to strip off her clothes, put on her pajamas, and collapse on the couch and do nothing.

The house was relatively quiet, but she could hear Max and the girls' voices through the heating vents, and she knew they were downstairs in the basement doing something.

"I'm home," she called, going to the basement door. When she received no answer, she simply continued unloading her car, letting the girls and Max continue with what they were doing.

As she sat the last bag of groceries on the kitchen counter, the doorbell rang. Wondering who was here now, she frowned, then went to open the door.

"Mrs. McCallister?" the uniformed young man said. "I have a delivery for Mrs. Sophie McCallister."

"I'm Sophie McCallister." He smiled, then lifted a long, white box and set it in her arms.

"I'll need you to sign for these," he said, reaching for a clipboard attached by a chain to his pants.

Sophie frowned at the white box. It was a traditional floral box and she couldn't imagine who on earth would be sending her flowers.

"Are you sure these are for me?" she asked, double checking the card.

"Yes, ma'am." He drew back and glanced at the address on the front of the house. "This is the correct address and they're for you. If you could just sign for them, please."

"Sure." She flashed him a smile, then dug in her jeans pocket for a tip. She found a dollar bill, handed it to him, thanked him, then shut the door, smiling in spite of herself. No one had sent her flowers since she'd been in high school.

Walking into the kitchen, Sophie set the box down on the table, and opened the card.

"Sophie, I can't wait for tonight. I'll pick you up at six. Our dinner reservations are for seven. Max."

"Reservations," Sophie muttered, staring at the card. Reservations meant a fancy restaurant, since she was pretty sure fast-food joints didn't require reservations. And a fancy restaurant meant she had to dress. Even though it had been years since she'd been in a fancy, elegant restaurant, even she knew she couldn't wear jeans and her traditional T-shirts.

Sophie slipped the cover off the floral box and her mouth fell open. "Oh my," she breathed, staring in awe at the incredibly beautiful long-stemmed white roses. There were exactly one dozen. One perfect dozen.

She lifted one white rose from its perch, sniffed its heavenly scent and felt all the fatigue seep out of her. The flowers were absolutely magnificent, and she pressed the white rose to her heart. She hadn't gotten flowers, let alone roses, from anyone in more years than she could remember.

Somehow, through all these years, Max had remembered that she'd once told him that white roses were her favorite flower in the world, and the one she thought the most romantic.

How on earth had he remembered something so trivial, she wondered, touched beyond measure.

Still pressing the beautiful stem to her heart, Sophie felt tears sting her eyes. This was the sweetest, most romantic gesture anyone had ever done for her.

She sniffed the flower again, then realized if Max was going to all this trouble to make their first date special, the least she could do was dress up.

She glanced at her watch, then frowned. He said he'd pick her up at six. Well, it was almost four forty-five now, and if she wanted to be ready, she was going to need a little help.

She hurriedly got a vase out of the cabinet, filled it with cold water, then carefully arranged the roses as well as the green flora and the spray of baby's breath into a breathtaking bouquet.

Once she was finished, she took the vase into the living room, setting it on a table right in front of the large picture window, before hurrying upstairs to her mother's room.

"Mom?" She knocked gently, then opened the door. Her mother was lying on her bed reading, but glanced up with a smile.

"So you're home finally," Carm said, setting her book down on the bed.

"Yeah, I am. The movies for tonight are on the television, and I told the girls earlier they could order a pizza since I knew I probably wouldn't get home in time to make one." Sophie hesitated, shifting from foot to foot. "Mom, do you think I could borrow something to wear tonight?" she asked hesitantly, stepping into the room. "And do you think you might help me do something with this hair?"

Sophie fluffed her unruly mane of black curls as her mother grinned at her.

"Darling, I thought you'd never ask." Carm slid off the bed and took her daughter's hand. "Come on in, dear. Together we'll make you irresistible."

Sophie sighed, grateful for her mother's maternal and feminine wisdom.

Chapter Five

Nervously, Max paced the length of Sophie's living room, glancing at his watch again and fiddling with his tie. He couldn't remember the last time he'd had a suit on so he'd gone out and bought a new one this afternoon, but then again, he couldn't remember the last time he'd courted a woman.

"You look great, Uncle Max," Mary said with a grin, tucking her bare toes under her nightgown as she curled up in one of the wing chairs.

"Yeah, real pretty," Carrie said with a grin of her own, curling her own bare toes under her as she snuggled closer to her sister in the same chair.

"Boys aren't pretty, Carrie," Mary said with a sniff. "They're handsome."

Carrie's chin lifted. "I don't care, I think Uncle Max is pretty anyway."

"Thanks, girls," Max said walking close to tweak both of their noses.

"Max. I'm sorry if I kept you waiting."

He turned toward the steps and his mouth dropped open. "Sophie?" He blinked in astonishment, certain he was seeing a vision. A beautiful, incredible vision.

Unable to take his eyes off her, his gaze widened, gliding over the beautiful woman descending down the stairs.

"Sophie, is that you?" As if in a trance, he walked to the bottom of the steps to simply watch her.

"It's me," she admitted with a laugh, self-consciously touching the dipping bodice of the slinky black evening dress her mother had loaned her. It was as simple as it was elegant. Unadorned, it fit her body like a second skin, dipping as low in front as it did in back, showing a great deal of creamy white skin and emphasizing her generous breasts, narrow waist, and long, shapely legs.

Fearing she might fall in her mother's enormously high heels, Sophie gripped the banister tightly, certain the four-inch black stiletto heels would send her tumbling headfirst at Max's feet. Hardly the elegant, sophisticated image she wanted to project tonight.

Absently, she also touched her curls. Her mother

had pinned up her hair with a beautiful hair clip, but styled several dozen loose curls to fall free, framing her face, which her mother had artfully made up with an array of cosmetics that emphasized her dark, smoky eyes, high cheekbones, and full, pouty lips. When she had looked in the mirror after her mother was finished, she couldn't believe it was her.

She no longer looked like a weary working mother, but like a sophisticated elegant woman ready for an exciting night on the town.

"I'm sorry if I kept you waiting," she said softly. She held out her hand to him—just as her mother had told her to do—and stepped off the last step.

Wide-eyed, Max took her hand and brought it to his mouth for a tender kiss.

"Sophie." Mesmerized, he said nothing more than her name, unable to form another coherent word or thought. Something deep and dark was stirring in his gut, something he knew he'd better get a handle on real quick if he didn't want to frighten Sophie.

She looked incredible. She'd always been a beautiful woman, but he'd never realized just how feminine and womanly she really was. He began to see her in a whole new light.

He kissed her hand again, inhaled her new scent, something smoky and so seductive it was almost intoxicating, and tried to clear his muddled mind. "You look astonishingly beautiful."

"Thank you." She flushed, trying not to reveal how her nerve endings were singing at his kiss, and the way he was looking at her. Not like his sister-in-law, but like a beautiful, desirable woman.

She couldn't remember the last time a man had looked at her that way and she felt the wonderful feminine tingle all the way to her toes.

"Mama, you look real pretty," Mary said.

"Doesn't she?" Carm said with pleasure, sweeping down the stairs in a black caftan and matching high-heeled marabou slippers.

"Yeah, Mama, you look real pretty," Carrie added, eyes shining as she scooted up on her knees to get a better look.

"Run along now, Max, Sophie," Carm said with a decided gleam in her eyes, enjoying the stunned look on Max's face and the reciprocal smile on her daughter's. "You don't want to be late for dinner."

"The car's waiting at the curb, Sophie," Max said, extending his arm to her as she grabbed the matching black shawl her mother had loaned her. Although the dress had long, slender sleeves, it was almost the end of October, and the night air was chilly with a hint of winter.

"Car?" Sophie repeated with a lift of her brow, slipping her arm through his.

He grinned. "I thought a limo might be appropriate. It's not every man who has to wait ten years for a date." He glanced at his watch. "But if we don't hurry, we'll be late for dinner." Opening the front door, he turned back to the girls and Carm. "Good night, guys. Don't wait up."

"Oh, darling, never fear, we'll be sound asleep long before you get home, I'm sure of it." Carm waved them off. "Have a wonderful time and stay safe."

As Max led Sophie toward the waiting car, she smiled, realizing this must have been how Cinderella felt on the way to the ball.

"Max, this has been a wonderful, enchanting evening." With a totally contented sigh, Sophie allowed herself to relax, and lean into Max, laying her head against his shoulder as he expertly led her around the small dance floor of the elegant supper club located in the heart of Chicago's downtown.

The famous club, known for its superb food and extraordinary service, featured autographed pictures of famous diners on the silk-lined walls, nestled comfortably alongside original, priceless works of art on loan from Chicago's Art Institute just a few blocks away.

The atmosphere was romantic and refined. The soft overhead lights were dimmed, while wall candelabras shimmered with golden amber light. The tables were small and intimate, adorned with lacy white linen tablecloths and small flickering candles.

Tucked discreetly in one marble-floored corner

was a small band, softly playing soothing romantic hits from decades gone by. .The marble floor extended out in a small, perfect circle, inviting dinner guests to take a spin to the wonderfully slow intoxicating music.

They'd devoured huge, fresh prawns nestled in a bed of tangy tartar sauce, followed by a Caesar salad, then finally filet mignons cooked to perfection, with a steaming baked potato dripping in butter, sour cream and chives.

Sophie couldn't remember when she'd had such a fantastic meal, or felt quite so satisfied.

Max's hand at her back sent shivers of awareness through her. Tonight, he no longer seemed like an indulgent, protective big brother, but something far more, something that she had to admit, both frightened and excited her.

Inhaling deeply, his cologne tickled her nose, her senses, making her so aware of him she nearly swooned. She'd always associated everything with Max as the ultimate in sexy masculinity.

And those eyes, she thought, dreamily, as their legs accidentally brushed against one another as he twirled her around the floor, were gorgeous. She'd seen those eyes register so many emotions. Joy and love whenever he looked at the girls. Kindness and patience when he was helping them with something. And desire when he looked at *her,* something she'd desperately been trying to ignore since he'd come home.

She had never seen desire in Max's eyes before, at least not since they first met, before they both realized that they simply weren't right for one another.

And she wasn't quite sure what to make of it.

Confused, all evening she'd watched him, wondering if the desire was real, or merely another part of his plan to get her to stop dating James.

Not knowing was making her a bit skittish to say the least. Desire was one emotion she was familiar with, at least with Max. She'd have been lying if she'd denied that desire was the first emotion she'd ever felt for Max. A desire that she'd buried so long ago.

She'd known from the day she met him he wasn't the kind of man who wanted to settle down or have a family, which was why he'd chosen the career he had, and why he continued to do his job.

But the knowledge that he'd actually been thinking of giving his high-flying lifestyle up for something a bit more stable and secure had made her wish that things could be different between them.

Sophie sighed a bit sadly. But it was impossible, she knew, because of who she was—his brother's widow—and who Max was. She'd never cease being Michael's widow to him and thus, forever off-limits for his own reasons of guilt and loyalty.

But still, Sophie thought dreamily, swaying along with him and letting her eyes slide closed so she could simply savor the wonderful feel of him pressed entirely against her, that didn't mean a woman couldn't dream.

"What are you smiling about?" Max whispered in her ear, almost making her jump in surprise. His soft breath fanned over the tender curve of her ear, drifting down toward her neck, sending a shiver racing down her spine and her pulse scrambling.

"Actually, Max, I was just thinking that someone should thank the person who taught you how to kiss." A tad embarrassed at being caught thinking about kissing him, she couldn't meet his eyes, instead, focusing on the starched pristine collar of his white shirt.

"Kiss?" he repeated with a lift of one brow. "You like the way I kiss?"

She laughed. "A woman would have to have been crazy not to like the way you kiss," she admitted, flushing beet-red.

"I see," he said, pressing his hand to her back, and swinging her around into his arms as the song ended. He slid both arms around her now, right in the middle of the dance floor.

She glanced up at him in confusion, saw the look on his face. Uh-oh. The tingle was back, right along the back of her neck at her hairline. What was the old saying about playing with fire? She had a feeling she should have thought about that before she'd made her offhanded comments. "Uh, Max, that was an observation, not an invitation," she commented.

"And do you really think I'm the kind of man who waits for an invitation to kiss a beautiful woman?" he asked, bending his head and brushing his lips teasingly against hers until she was all but clinging to the front of his lapels.

"Max." Her voice squeaked out as he gathered her even closer. Embarrassed, Sophie glanced around, aware of the other couples walking off the dance floor, discreetly smiling at them. "We're standing in the middle of a dance floor in front of a hundred people."

Smiling, he continued to draw her close, until her body was pressed intimately against his. They fit so perfectly together, she realized dully, as she felt his hard masculine heat press against her in a way that reminded her very vividly that in spite of being alone for so very many years she was still very much a young woman with feelings and desires.

"And your point is?" he whispered against her mouth. His lips were gentle and seductive, working playfully, tenderly at hers, slowly caressing, brushing to and fro until her breath was nearly panting out of her. Heat soared through her until her skin felt as if it had been electrically charged.

With her mind dulled and her senses acutely alive,

Sophie blinked at him as his mouth continued to arouse and seduce.

"Max." His name whispered out of her mouth a fraction of a moment before his mouth covered hers entirely, lightly, gently, and then, finding welcome, became more demanding until she was on tiptoe, ignorant of where they were or who might be watching.

The floor seemed to tilt right under her feet, and she clung to him, aware only of the man in her arms and the sensations rampaging through her.

Max's hands, soft, gentle and so warm, roamed her back, igniting a fire everywhere they touched. The material of her dress was merely a thin barrier, no match for skin heated by desire. Another soft moan slipped from her lips as his hands slid to her waist to mold her to him, then lower still to gently caress the curve of her hips.

Her nipples began to ache beneath the material of her dress, and Sophie desperately clung to him as arousal and desire made her legs weak and wobbly.

She'd reacted to Max like long dried kindling to a match, she thought hesitantly, tightening her arms around his neck, slipping her fingers into the soft silk of his hair, wanting—needing him even closer. But it wasn't just physical, she thought hazily. She reacted to Max on every level.

And it simply terrified her.

She could handle him when he was merely playing the role of the protective big brother, but this…this man she'd seen today was someone she wasn't entirely sure she could handle.

Max groaned softly when he felt Sophie's entire body tremble against him. He heard her sigh, felt her lips warm and give under his.

It had been so long since he'd been on an official date with a woman so he'd had no idea if he'd even remember how it went. His past relationships, because of his job, usually never lasted past a night, and surely nothing as official as a "date."

But with Sophie, everything just seemed to come naturally. But then again it always had.

Maybe because he'd waited more than ten long years to even be able to *allow* himself to think of her this way, to touch her this way, but more importantly, to *want* her this way.

Guilt came, as it always did. She was, after all his brother's widow, but how much longer did he have to deny himself everything that mattered to him in life?

Everything he'd forgone so that his brother Michael could have what he'd always wanted, needed?

And then when Michael *had* everything in the world, he'd simply thrown it all away as if it were meaningless.

As the older of the twins, it was Max's job to take care of his brother. And he took his responsibilities seriously, and always had.

Michael's inability to conceive had seemed to have eaten him alive. He began drinking and acting belligerent, making Sophie fear for her marriage.

It had been a call from Sophie, begging Max to help Michael, to help her that had brought about their arrangement.

Max and Michael had made a pact; a solemn vow between brothers. Max would father Michael's child through artificial insemination because a childhood bout of mumps had left Michael sterile, but once it was done, they would never speak of it aloud for the child's sake.

Max could never acknowledge the child as his own, nor could he ever claim it as his own. Michael would always be acknowledged and recognized as the baby's father.

But the baby had turned out to be *babies,* beautiful, breathtaking twin miracles that had captured Max's heart and his soul the moment he'd laid eyes on their tiny little faces.

He couldn't bear the thought that the woman he'd secretly cared for all these years had given birth to *his* children—children he could never claim.

Regrets were many, but far too late. The damage—the deed—had been done. Not that he'd ever regret for a minute the twin miracles he'd given life to.

No one had expected Michael to die, leaving Sophie a widow and the twins fatherless. It had only complicated things for Max. As well, no doubt, for Sophie.

Dear Sophie.

Max tightened his arms around her, took the kiss deeper, as if his presence alone could erase all the pain, hurt and rejection she and the girls had needlessly endured because of Michael.

Once Sophie had conceived, Michael hadn't been able to accept or get over the fact that he hadn't been able to father his own children. Max was never sure whether it was pride or ego that had fueled his brother's anger and self-loathing, but whatever it was, it was enough to almost bring all of them down.

Max couldn't understand why Michael couldn't appreciate the blessings he'd been bestowed with— a beautiful loving wife, beautiful twin daughters, a home of his own—blessings Max would have killed for.

Instead, Michael blamed Sophie, resented her, and finally, ultimately rejected the twins with his coldness.

Max knew it had nearly killed Sophie to watch Michael behave like that toward her precious daughters, especially since the entire artificial insemination plan had been Michael's idea in the first place. But Michael had simply thrown it all away, nearly destroying everyone else in the process.

When the twins were barely three years old Michael had gotten drunk, then got behind the wheel of his car on an icy, snowy day. When Michael's car had skidded over the guard rail, he'd been killed instantly.

It was ruled a vehicular accident.

But Max and Sophie suspected differently, although they'd never discussed it. Like the circumstances of the twins' birth, it was one of those things that they simply couldn't discuss because it would open a Pandora's box of issues that he wasn't sure either of them were fully prepared to deal with.

He'd gone to Chicago when Michael had died, but he held his tongue and his heart. Hurting and aching for Sophie, wanting only to comfort and protect her and the girls, he knew it wasn't the time to approach her, to tell her how he felt about her, about *his* daughters. And he had no idea what the impact would be on Sophie or the girls.

So, once again he fled, knowing if he didn't, he might do something that would forever alienate Sophie.

He knew he had to give her some time to heal, and so he bided his time, playing the affectionate, overprotective and doting uncle—until the twins' message came about Beardsley.

He had to admit it had nearly sent him into a tailspin, the thought of another man claiming Sophie and *his* daughters.

Not on a bet, he thought firmly, holding Sophie closer, tighter.

So he'd come home to finally claim his daughters and the woman he loved more than life itself.

Now, he just had to figure out exactly how to do that without destroying the trust they'd built, the loyalty that came from their agreement, and more importantly his relationship with Sophie as well as with his daughters.

"Max." Breathless and shaking, Sophie drew back from him, blinking at the soft lights surrounding her, realizing they were the center of attention.

Max found himself blinking back at her. He'd been lost in a haze of memories and lust, lost, and not particularly anxious to find his way back.

"The music has started again, and we're…uh… cluttering up the dance floor, to say nothing of making a public spectacle of ourselves," Sophie said a bit self-consciously. Pressing a hand to her racing heart, she waited a moment until her legs steadied before stepping out of Max's arms.

"Spoilsport," he said with a smile, draping an arm around her waist and leading her off the dance floor. "Would you like another drink, Sophie, or perhaps some dessert?" Max asked as he pulled out her chair for her. He'd been as shaken as she by the kiss, not wanting it to end.

She glanced up with a smile. "No, thanks, Max." Nervously, she touched the napkin that she'd left folded on the table. She needed something to do with her hands, and some time to think things through and figure out what was going on here with Max.

And with her heart.

And she certainly couldn't do that when Max was touching her, kissing her, or holding her in his arms.

"Tired?" he asked sympathetically as he pulled his own chair out and sat down.

"A bit." Sophie suddenly remembered something. "Max?"

His gaze was steady on hers and seeing the confusion and concern in her eyes, he reached across the table and took her hands in his.

"Yes, Sophie?"

"I never thanked you for the roses." Her smile bloomed at the thought of the beautiful stems. She leaned across the table a bit, giving his hands an affectionate squeeze. "How on earth did you ever remember white roses were my favorite flowers?"

"Because I remember you telling me once that they were," he said with a careless shrug.

"Yes, but Max, that had to be what? Nine or ten years ago." Her brows drew together a bit. "That was probably even before Michael and I got married. How on earth could you remember something as insignificant like that?"

He met her gaze, and the look on his face, so dark, so intense, sent a shiver racing over her. "I always remember things that are important to me, Sophie," he said quietly, lifting their linked fingers to his lips, to softly brush a kiss over hers. She felt the impact of his kiss all the way to her toes, which curled in her shoes.

"You never fail to surprise me," she said, leaning back to look at his face.

"And you never fail to surprise me." He felt a thrill when he heard her sigh of contentment. "Did you have a good time tonight?"

"I had a wonderful time," she admitted with a grin, thinking of the way she'd felt when she was in his arms. She couldn't quite remember the last time she'd wanted a man to hold her like this, or made her feel like this.

He grinned, relieved. "This dating thing isn't so bad now, is it?"

"No." Content, she sighed again. "It's not," she admitted a bit reluctantly.

So why hadn't she felt this relaxed and content when she was with James? All she felt with James was nervous.

"Good, because I think it's something we should do again."

"Again?" she repeated. "Max," Sophie began carefully, pleating the end of her napkin with nervous fingers. "Do you want to tell me exactly what you're up to?"

"Well, Sophie, in case you haven't noticed, what I'm up to is wooing you."

"Wooing me?" she said in surprise. "But why?"

"I'm wooing you, Sophie, because it's time."

"Time?" she repeated in confusion, still not understanding.

"Yeah, Sophie." He brought her hands to his mouth for a kiss. "It's *my* time, Sophie. And I intend to take full advantage of it."

Chapter Six

By midweek, the temperatures outdoors had dropped significantly, reminding Max what winter in the Midwest was like.

But all the boards and materials necessary for the girls' basement playroom had been delivered and were now stacked up in a corner of the basement so he had plenty to keep him busy.

He'd been running up and down, tape measure around his neck, tool belt around his waist grumbling and mumbling and simply throwing himself into his task.

It had been a very long time since he'd actually done any physical or manual labor, other than lifting and loading a camera, and to Max's surprise he found he enjoyed this—sore shoulder and still-aching ribs notwithstanding.

He'd drawn up the plans himself. For a project this small there wasn't much to it and it certainly wasn't difficult. Then he'd passed it by Sophie and the girls for their approval.

He'd decided to separate the large basement into two sections. One would be an actual playroom with shelves covering one entire wall for all the girls' books and their toys. And the other room he was outfitting with a wall-length mirror, wooden plank floors and a ballet barre against one wall so the girls could practice. He was also going to add some heavy-weight floor mats as well—just so the girls didn't hurt themselves if they stumbled, or tumbled.

The playroom was coming along and he anticipated finishing it within two to three weeks at best—and that was *with* the girls' help.

Without it, he probably could have had it done in a week to ten days at best. But it was worth having their input and their company, worth it to see the pride in their faces at having worked at something they were proud of, he thought with an indulgent smile.

They were terrific kids. And they deserved only the very best life had to offer. And that included a father, he thought firmly, swiping sweat off his forehead with the back of his hand as he went in search of another board.

"Max?" Sophie's voice drifted down the stairs toward him and he straightened, glancing toward the stairs.

"Yeah?"

"You've got a phone call."

Max scowled, swiping his forehead again. He had no idea what time it was, but it had to be late. The girls had gone to bed at least an hour ago. So who the heck was calling him this late? he wondered, his frown deepening.

Remembering he'd stopped by the architect's office this afternoon to discuss the *other* plans he'd wanted drawn up, the ones for the carriage house out back, Max thought better of asking Sophie to take a message.

Her surprise wouldn't be much of a surprise if it were the architect on the phone.

Starting up the stairs, he pushed open the basement door, and glanced up. Sophie was dressed in a warm, comfortable jogging suit the color of bright lemons, and her hair was piled atop her head. And there was, he noted with a grin, a pencil sticking out of it.

She was standing there with his cell phone in her hand. Whenever he went in the basement to work, he left it with her in case he received any calls.

"Thanks," he said, taking the phone from her and

giving her a quick but satisfying kiss. "Nice glasses," he teased, pulling back from her and covering the receiver with his hand as she flushed, shook her head as if to clear it, then turned to walk back into the living room.

He'd been teasing her about her thick black reading glasses since he'd come home, unaware that she even wore glasses. Letting his gaze longingly follow the sweet little sway of her rear in her baggy jogging suit as she walked out of the kitchen, Max smiled, then leaned wearily against the kitchen counter, absently rubbing his aching shoulder.

"Max McCallister," he said into the phone. "How ya doing Sam?" he asked, recognizing his attorney's voice. "You don't say?" Fascinated, Max began to pace, listening intently to his attorney, trying not to get excited.

Take it slow, he cautioned himself, still listening intently. He needed to make sure he thought every single aspect of this new business proposal through thoroughly if he was going to make all of this work for all of them.

And it had to work, he thought, resuming his pacing. For all their sakes.

In the living room, Sophie poked at the fire, stoking it then watching it flare before sinking back down on the couch. She reached for her afghan, trying to concentrate on her midterm progress reports

GET FREE BOOKS and a FREE GIFT WHEN YOU PLAY THE...

Just scratch off the silver box with a coin. Then check below to see the gifts you get!

SLOT MACHINE GAME!

YES! I have scratched off the silver box. Please send me the 2 free Silhouette Special Edition® books and gift for which I qualify. I understand I am under no obligation to purchase any books, as explained on the back of this card.

335 SDL D354

235 SDL D36L

FIRST NAME

LAST NAME

ADDRESS

APT.#

CITY

STATE/PROV.

ZIP/POSTAL CODE

7	7	7	**Worth TWO FREE BOOKS plus a BONUS Mystery Gift!**
🍒	🍒	🍒	**Worth TWO FREE BOOKS!**
♣	♣	♣	**Worth ONE FREE BOOK!**
🔔	🔔	🔔	**TRY AGAIN!**

www.eHarlequin.com

(S-SE-12/04)

DETACH AND MAIL CARD TODAY!

The Silhouette Reader Service™ — Here's how it works:

Accepting your 2 free books and gift places you under no obligation to buy anything. You may keep the books and gift and return the shipping statement marked "cancel." If you do not cancel, about a month later we'll send you 6 additional books and bill you just $4.24 each in the U.S., or $4.99 each in Canada, plus 25¢ shipping & handling per book and applicable taxes if any.* That's the complete price and — compared to cover prices of $4.99 each in the U.S. and $5.99 each in Canada — it's quite a bargain! You may cancel at any time, but if you choose to continue, every month we'll send you 6 more books, which you may either purchase at the discount price or return to us and cancel your subscription.
*Terms and prices subject to change without notice. Sales tax applicable in N.Y. Canadian residents will be charged applicable provincial taxes and GST. Credit or debit balances in a customer's account(s) may be offset by any other outstanding balance owed by or to the customer.

934

96-34 35 32 17

BUSINESS REPLY MAIL

FIRST-CLASS MAIL   PERMIT NO. 717-003   BUFFALO, NY

POSTAGE WILL BE PAID BY ADDRESSEE

SILHOUETTE READER SERVICE
3010 WALDEN AVE
PO BOX 1867
BUFFALO NY 14240-9952

NO POSTAGE
NECESSARY
IF MAILED
IN THE
UNITED STATES

for the parent-teacher conferences she had every night this week. Her mind wasn't on her work. It was in the kitchen—on Max's phone call.

With a weary sigh, she leaned back against the couch, tucked her legs under her and merely stared at the fire.

She hated to admit it, but she was beginning to feel like Cinderella. Her days were still harried and frantic, rushing to get herself and the girls ready and off to school in the morning, then teaching all day, coming home weary and exhausted.

But then her evenings were spent with Max.

It was such a delight to find someone waiting for her every night when she got home from work, anxious to hear about her day, or her problems. And she found herself looking forward to the end of the day, knowing Max would be there.

Every evening after homework and dinner, Max and the girls would troop upstairs or downstairs and make themselves scarce until it was almost time for bed, then Max would spend the rest of the evening with her. And she couldn't help but look forward to this time in the evening when the girls were in bed, and Max was done working downstairs.

For the first time since her daughters' birth, she finally knew and understood what it meant to have a true partner, because in just a short time, Max had become just that.

Sometimes they just talked, sometimes they

curled up together on the couch and watched a
movie. And sometimes they did nothing but merely
watch the fire in the fireplace and munch on homemade popcorn simply enjoying each other's company.

She was getting used to having Max there, she
realized a bit nervously. She was getting accustomed
to leaning on Max, to depending on him and his
presence. And that was dangerous. And she knew it.

And if she'd forgotten how dangerous, his phone
call tonight would have served as a vivid reminder.

Just like every other time before when Max had
come home, once the phone calls started arriving,
the days until Max once again left were numbered.

With a sigh, Sophie tucked the afghan a bit more
tightly around her, trying to stay warm as she
searched through her papers and folders for her pencil. This big old house was literally as drafty as a
barn, especially in the winter when the wind blew
in from the lake.

"Sophie?"

She glanced up to find Max standing in the living
room. "Are you leaving?" she blurted without
thinking.

"Leaving?" he repeated with a frown that turned
into a grin when he realized she was searching for
her pencil. He walked over to her and pulled it loose
from her hair. "I just got here," he said, handing

her the pencil. "Don't tell me you're anxious to get rid of me already?" he asked worriedly.

"No." She shook her head. "Of course not. I...I...was just...wondering."

He nodded, a faraway look in his eyes. "Sophie, I need to ask you something."

"Ask away."

He shifted his weight. "You know the carriage house out back? The one no one uses?"

Her brows drew together. "Yeah?" she said carefully. "What about it?"

"Would you be willing to rent it to me?"

"Rent it to you?" She laughed. "Max, there's no heat in there. It's practically falling down because no one has done any work in there in ages. Why on earth would you want to rent it?"

"Let's just say I've got a project I'm working on and I'm going to need that space." He flashed her a grin. "So what do you say? Will you rent it to me?"

She shrugged. "No, I won't rent it to you. But you can use it for whatever or however long you need to."

"You're sure?" he asked.

"Positive. No one's using it anyway, Max. But be forewarned, like I said, there's no heat in there, no electricity and no plumbing. As the days progress, deeper into winter it's going to get colder and colder, making it nearly uninhabitable."

"That's fine," Max said amiably. "I'll take care of that." He and the architect had already discussed calling in a contractor to install heat, plumbing, and electricity. "So, it's a deal?"

"Yes, it's a deal."

"Good. There'll probably be some workmen coming in and out of there for the next few weeks, so just don't get alarmed."

"Just make sure you keep the girls out of there while you're working. I don't even think the floorboards are secure and I don't want them getting hurt," Sophie said.

"You got it," he said, wearily rubbing his aching shoulder again.

"Is your shoulder bothering you again?" she asked, concerned.

He nodded. "A bit."

"You need to ice it, Max. And maybe give it a rest for a few days. You've been working in the basement nonstop and it just might be too much too soon."

"Yeah, maybe you're right, but I want to get the girls' playroom finished as soon as possible." He glanced at the fire, rubbing his shoulder again. "I think I'll close up downstairs and call it a night." He glanced at the stack of her paperwork on the couch. "You about done for the night?"

She was now. "Yeah, just about."

"Good. Why don't you open a bottle of wine and

make some popcorn, and I'll go close up downstairs."

"Okay." Sophie unwound her legs, moved the afghan and stood up.

"I'll meet you right here in about ten minutes, okay?"

She nodded, worrying her lower lip as she watched him walk away. Maybe he wasn't leaving *yet,* but he would, soon, and Sophie knew she had to fortify her defenses and protect her heart, because if she didn't when Max left, her heart would be broken.

And this time she wasn't quite certain there was anything she could do to stop it.

By the end of the week, the girls had become nearly giddy about the Halloween festival.

On Friday afternoon, shortly after her last class of the day, Sophie was hurrying down the hall, clutching a batch of student papers and files, on her way to her office.

The girls and Max had promised they'd have a surprise for her this afternoon after school and she was now anxious to get home.

"Sophie? Sophie, dear, just a moment."

Sophie stopped and almost groaned when she heard James's voice behind her. She really didn't have time to stop and chat right now. She had too many things to do before she got home. She hadn't seen James outside of school since Max had arrived, and immediately felt guilty for her thoughts.

He'd been so kind to her the past six months it simply wasn't fair not to return the kindness.

Planting a smile on her face, she turned to him in the hallway, forcing herself to be cheerful. "Hi, James. How are you?"

He hurried up to her, smoothing down first his hair and then his collar. "Fine. Fine, dear. Unfortunately I've been so busy preparing for the festival tonight as well as student conferences I haven't had much of an opportunity to see you. How are you?"

"I'm fine, James," she said with a smile. "But just as busy."

"Why don't we step into my office for a moment. There's something I need to discuss with you," James said, glancing up and down the nearly empty corridor.

"Okay," Sophie said with a frown, allowing him to lead her toward his office, which was just down the hall.

Since it was Friday, most of the administrative staff as well as the teachers had left as soon as they could, leaving the building all but abandoned.

Sophie followed James through his administrative assistant's office, then into his own, setting her file folders down on an empty chair and taking the other.

"You're looking well as usual," James said, taking a seat behind his large, slightly battered desk.

"Thank you," she said a bit impatiently, wondering what was on his mind and hoping he'd get on with it.

"Well, dear, I was just wondering…" He glanced down at his desk, then at her. "I was wondering if you're still going to attend the Halloween festival with me this evening?"

"Oh James, I'm so sorry," Sophie said, leaning closer. She shook her head. "Quite frankly, with Max home for a visit, it completely slipped my mind." Which was true. She'd totally forgotten she'd promised James she'd attend the festival with him. "I really am sorry, James, but since Max comes to visit so infrequently I don't think it would be fair to have me just leave him on his own." Nor did she want to, she realized. This was the first time in a long time they were attending the festival as a family and she knew how excited the girls were about it and how much they were looking forward to it. She wouldn't dare disappoint them now.

"Yes, well, that's perfectly understandable," James said with a gracious smile. "In fact, I understand perfectly."

"You do?" Sophie said in surprise. She'd expected James to be at least at little annoyed that for the moment, at least while Max was home, she simply wasn't going to be able to continue to see him. To be honest, she was no longer certain she even wanted to.

"Yes, I do," he said, his smile going wider. "In fact, I know it's very important for Max to spend time with the girls. As you've told me, you and the girls are the only family he has left."

"That's true," Sophie said, relieved at how well James seemed to be taking this.

"That's why I think we should take advantage of this opportunity, dear."

"What opportunity?" Sophie asked with a frown, not following him.

"Well, I know this wonderful bed-and-breakfast in Lake Geneva. It's only about an hour and a half from here, and I thought while Max was here, and since he wants to spend so much time with the girls, it would be the perfect opportunity for you and I to get away for the weekend."

Sophie simply stared at him. "Excuse me?"

James sat forward, carefully adjusting the sleeves of his suit jacket. "Yes, well, Sophie, as I was saying, I think leaving Max alone with the girls for the weekend is a wonderful opportunity—"

"Did you just ask me to go away with you for the *weekend?*" Sophie asked, her voice rising in both shock and anger.

"Why, yes. I thought it might be a splendid time—"

"No." Fueled by anger and by James's sheer audacity, Sophie surged to her feet so abruptly, she almost knocked her chair backward, but she caught it just in time.

"Yes, well, then, if next weekend isn't good for you, dear, I'm sure I can rearrange our reservations." James frowned slightly. "But this resort is extremely popular—it might be difficult as the holidays get closer."

Clutching her files tightly to her, Sophie said, "I'm sorry, but it's just not possible." She started to turn to leave before she said or did something she would regret, but he hurried around his desk and caught her arm before she got to the door.

She looked down at his hand, then slowly lifted her gaze to his. "James," she said through clenched teeth, angry and more annoyed than she'd been in a long time.

What on earth had ever given him the idea she was interested in getting to know him *that* much better?

She quickly thought over her words, deeds and actions since she'd started this stupid dating experiment and realized she hadn't done anything to lead James on.

"James. We've been out several times in a group of teachers, and had one date. I hardly think that qualifies for a weekend away alone together. I thought I'd made myself perfectly clear when I agreed to go out with you about why and how I expected things to proceed, if they proceed at all."

"Well, yes, you did. Quite clearly, dear." His brows drew together. "Perhaps I'm moving too fast, then?" he said and she wanted to roll her eyes, wondering what on earth was his first *clue?*

"Too *fast?*" Sophie didn't know whether to scream in frustration or simply laugh. Then remembering James was still her boss and she needed her job, she reined in the hot words that nearly burned her tongue.

"Yes, James, I'd say that might be a classic understatement." She yanked open his office door, anxious to get out of there.

"We'll simply plan on another weekend then," he said to her retreating back. "I'll be happy to reschedule our reservations. I'll still see you tonight at the festival, won't I?" James asked, not at all rejected by her rebuff.

"Oh, I'll be there," she confirmed over her shoulder. "With my family," she added firmly.

"Good. Good." Gallant as ever, he waved to her as Sophie marched down the hall. "I'll see you tonight then, dear."

Sophie didn't even bother to turn around.

He'd see her tonight?

Sophie wanted to sigh, realizing the only person she really wanted to see tonight was Max.

By the time Sophie got home, she was still simmering in indignation, but her anger disappeared the moment she pulled in the driveway and saw her beautiful daughters as well as her surprise.

"Mama! Mama! Watch me!" Grinning from ear to ear, Carrie carefully steered her pink two-wheeler without training wheels down the sidewalk. "Look what Uncle Max taught me! Look, Mama! I can ride my bike all by myself." With her helmet firmly in place, along with knee and elbow pads, Carrie bit her lower lip in concentration as she clutched the handle bars tightly. The bars wobbled ferociously for a moment, causing Sophie to hold her breath in fear, pressing a hand to her thundering heart.

But Max was right behind Carrie, encouraging her, a look of pleasure and pride on his face, as he stood close enough to catch Carrie if she started to fall, but far enough away to give Carrie a feeling of independence.

"That's wonderful, sweetheart," she called to Carrie with a wave as she got out of the car, as her daughter continued her wobbly ride down the sidewalk. All by herself. "Absolutely wonderful."

It was foolish to cry, Sophie thought with a sniffle. But it was just that her little girls were growing up so fast. One day they were babies, the next they were getting on the school bus, and now they were riding bikes on their own. The next thing she knew they'd be driving cars and dating boys. She couldn't even contemplate her precious babies dating boys.

Male…*creatures*.

Oh, God.

Remembering her uncomfortable encounter with James, Sophie almost shivered. She didn't think as a mother she was ready to even go there. Her mind backpedaled, erasing all thoughts of boys, and concentrating once again on training wheels and two-wheelers, which was far safer.

"I can ride by myself, too, Mama," Mary said, racing up to Sophie and taking her hand. Sophie grabbed her daughter in a hug, then smacked a loud kiss to the top of her head, filled with joy at these beautiful miracles she'd created.

"You can?" Sophie said with a laugh. "How long have you two been practicing?" She'd promised the girls she'd teach them to ride their two-wheelers without training wheels next summer. But she had to admit, the idea had been daunting since she feared the girls falling and getting hurt.

"Uncle Max has been helping us for almost a week now." Mary swung her mother's hand to and fro, then lifted her other hand to scratch her head under her own pink safety helmet. "Every day, after our snack and before we start our homework Uncle Max comes out here with us and helps us. We learn real good, Mama. Uncle Max said so."

"I can see that," Sophie said, glancing at Max and feeling a well of gratitude and warmth toward him. "I'm so proud of you," Sophie said, giving her daughter another hug. "Both of you." Grinning,

Sophie stepped away from her car, her papers and files forgotten as she headed toward Carrie who had almost steered herself—with Max's expert help— right back in front of the house.

"Look at you," Sophie said, when Carrie brought the bike to a rather shaky halt in front of the front porch. "Look at how grown up you are, baby." Sophie lifted a grinning Carrie off the bike and twirled her around. "I'm so proud of you, sweetheart."

Beaming with pride, Carrie said, "Thank you, Mama, but Uncle Max helped me."

"So I hear," Sophie said, her gaze going over Carrie's head to meet Max's. He was holding onto Carrie's bike, pride and pleasure shining in his eyes and not for the first time Sophie thought what a truly wonderful father he'd have made.

Oh, Max.

A sad, sharp ache settled somewhere deep in her heart, in that place she'd kept hidden from everyone for so very long.

They'd cheated Max out of so much, she thought, her heart aching. And he'd willingly sacrificed so much for his brother, a brother who hadn't even bothered to ever thank him or appreciate what a truly wonderful and generous gift he'd been given.

But she'd never forgotten, never failed to appreciate the precious gift they'd been given—because of Max. Dear Max.

Sophie ached to hold Max and let him know that his gift had not been unappreciated.

If it wasn't for Max, she wouldn't have these beautiful twin miracles.

"Max." Nearly overcome with emotion, her eyes filled as she reached for him, nearly squashing Carrie between them. "Thank you," she whispered, drawing him close and wrapping her arms tightly around him as Carrie scooted out of the way and raced off toward her sister who was climbing on her own pink bike.

"For what?" he asked in surprise, not wanting to look a gift horse in the mouth, but not certain exactly what Sophie was thanking him for—or hugging him for.

For my children, she thought silently. *For my beautiful precious little girls.*

"For…everything," she said. Ignoring the hot tears that stung her eyes, Sophie met his gaze, and held it despite what it was doing to her insides. "Thank you, dear Max, for everything."

He slid his arms around her waist, his gaze never leaving hers. "My dearest Sophie," he whispered. "You're more than welcome." In spite of the fact that the girls were just a few feet away, Max lowered his head and kissed Sophie, relishing her soft heady sigh, and the way her arms slid around him, slowly and reluctantly at first, and then higher, tighter, as if accepting him and welcoming him.

It was the most wonderful feeling in the world, he thought, to have the mother of your children, the woman you'd always loved...want and welcome you.

"Uncle Max." Carrie tugged on his pants. "Uncle Max, are you kissing Mama?"

Trying not to laugh, Max drew back, his gaze never leaving Sophie's. "Yeah, honey, I guess I am," he said, keeping his arms around Sophie to keep her close. The girls might as well get used to him kissing their mother, he decided, because he intended to make a practice of it. A *regular* practice.

Frowning, Carrie asked, "How come?"

"Grown-ups always kiss," Mary announced, coming up to them, swinging their helmets and safety pads in her hands.

"How come?" Carrie persisted, turning her attention to her sister.

"Dunno," Mary said, shrugging. "But grown-ups are always smooching on television," she added with a giggle.

"Weird," Carrie said with a frown. She looked up at her mother and her uncle. "If you're done kissing now, could we eat dinner? We're hungry."

Laughing, Max leaned his forehead against Sophie's, realizing he was content.

By the time they arrived at the Halloween festival, the gymnasium was filled almost to capacity. Packed to the rafters with children dressed in gaily colored costumes, the room was decorated with orange-and-black streamers, balloons and colored lights. Divided into several different sections, there were booths with various foods, booths for apple dunking, booths for face painting, and a booth for "dunking the principal." One whole section of the gym was cordoned off as a haunted house for the children. Proceeds from all of the events would go toward the library book fund to buy much-needed new books for the school library.

"This is absolutely incredible," Max said and grinned in delight as he glanced around.

Touched by the look on his face, Sophie smiled at him. "Max, it's just a Halloween festival. We have one just like it every year." She hesitated a moment before turning back to him. "You've never been to a Halloween festival, have you?" she asked softly, her heart aching at the thought.

"Nope," he said with a grin, still glancing around. "Growing up in a group home didn't allow for much holiday celebrations, and when Michael and I were in the foster home, well…" His voice trailed off and he shrugged, not wanting to talk about it.

Sophie, who was holding Mary's hand while Max held Carrie's, slipped her free hand in his and gave him a comforting squeeze. He'd missed so much, she thought sadly, not just as a child, but as an adult as well. It made her unbearably sad. "Well then, Max, you're in for a treat. District 203 is well-known for its fabulous celebrations and festivals, so if this is your first, you picked a good one."

Frowning, Max glanced around again feeling a bit skittish at the crowd. "Sophie, there's so many people here, how on earth do you keep track of the girls?" He tightened his hand on Carrie's. The thought of losing the girls in this crowd was just a bit intimidating.

"I'll let you in on a mother's secret," she said with a smile. "Girls?"

Wide-eyed and trying to take everything in, the girls looked up at her. "Yes, Mama?" Mary said as Carrie swiveled her neck back and forth still trying to see everything.

"Explain to Uncle Max the rules for when we're in a crowd."

Mary blinked, then shifted her gaze to her uncle's. "Uncle Max, we have to hold Mama's hand—"

"And each other's," Carrie injected with a grin.

"That's so we don't lose one another—"

"Or get lost."

Pleased, Sophie smiled proudly at them. "And if something should happen and one of us should get lost. Or we get separated, what do we do, girls?"

"We go to the lost place," both girls said.

"What's the lost place?" Max asked, glancing

from the girls to Sophie who chuckled at the look on his face.

"It's a place that we designate as soon as we get somewhere. We pick out a place to meet in case we get separated or lost." Sophie glanced around. "Girls, do you see the water fountain over there? It's right there near the girls' washroom." Sophie pointed and three pairs of eyes followed the movement of her hand. "That's the designated lost place tonight. If we get separated or lost, don't get scared, simply go stand by the water fountain and wait for me or Uncle Max to find you." Sophie hesitated a moment. "And what's the cardinal rule, girls?"

"Once you get to the lost place you don't leave until Mama comes to get you," Carrie said solemnly as Mary shook her head.

"That's right." Sophie beamed as she glanced around. "Okay, so what do you want to do first?" She laughed as the girls and Max all started talking at once. "Okay, okay, why don't we split up? Max, why don't you take Carrie over to the apple dunking booth, since that's where she wants to go first, and I'll take Mary over to the face painting booth."

"Can I get my face painted when I'm done dunking for apples, Mama?"

"Yes, Carrie." Sophie bent and kissed the top of her daughter's head. "You be good and listen to Uncle Max, okay?"

Carrie bobbed her head solemnly, eyes wide in awe at all the activity and people around her.

"And Max?"

"Yes?" Jostled by a group of kids running and not watching where they were going, Max instinctively moved closer to Carrie.

"Don't let go of Carrie's hand," she cautioned. "The girls get excited and want to run ahead, but that's not allowed when we're in a crowd this large."

"No kidding," he said with a frown, deciding he'd feel better if he carried Carrie. With one swift motion, he lifted her in his arms to carry her. "This way I'll be sure not to lose her."

Sophie laughed. "That will work for the first hour. Then when your arms get tired, she'll need to walk, so just remember the rules."

"I will," he said.

Sophie glanced at her watch. "Okay, we'll meet right here in about an hour. Is that enough time?" She looked at Max and he shrugged.

"I guess so, but remember, I'm a novice at this, so whatever you say is fine."

"Good." Impulsively, Sophie leaned forward and kissed Max on the cheek. "Have fun. We'll see you in a hour."

"Psst. Uncle Max, hide me. Quick." Eyes wide with fright, Carrie clenched the back of her uncle's jeans as they made their way through the crowd toward the booth where kids could pay a dollar and then throw a softball at a booth to try to dunk the principal. It was one of the most popular booths in the place.

Tonight was the first time in Max's life he could ever remember doing a "family" thing and he couldn't remember a time he'd enjoyed himself more. After the first hour, he and Carrie had met up with Sophie and Mary. He'd eaten old-fashioned popcorn balls, shared several pieces of fudge with Sophie, had a very frightening-looking skeleton painted on his cheek, courtesy of one of the school artists, and had simply enjoyed himself, watching the joy and delight the girls experienced as they made their way through and around all the wonderful booths. Now, as they were getting ready to go home for the evening, Sophie had taken Mary over to get her face painted. It was the first time in the last couple of hours the line had shortened. Max had agreed to take Carrie over to the principal's dunking booth while Sophie and Mary continued to wait in line.

"Hide you?" Confused, Max turned to Carrie, surprised to find her cowering behind his pant leg. "Carrie, sweetheart." Concerned, he went down on his knees next to her, cradling her in his arms to protect her from the crowd. "What's wrong?"

Silently, Carrie pointed across the gymnasium.

"It's him," she whispered, her eyes going round and wide. "Mr. Bugs-bee. He's coming over to us." Carrie's frightened gaze darted across the gym then back again. "You have to hide me."

Max turned, saw James smiling and glad-handing his way across the gymnasium toward them, and Max sighed. "Sweetheart, stop hiding." Gently, Max pried Carrie loose from behind him. "There's nothing for you to be afraid of. He's not going to hurt you, sweetheart," Max said firmly, stroking a comforting hand down her cheek. He lifted one brow. "Do you really think Uncle Max would let anything happen to you? Or let him hurt you?"

She shook her head, sending her dark bob flying around her face. "But what if he yells at me again?" Carrie asked, looking up at him with wide, innocent eyes.

"Sweetheart, I promise he's not going to yell at you ever again. Do you understand?" She merely stared at him wide-eyed. "Don't be afraid. I promise you nothing will happen. Honest." Max kissed her cheek. "Have I ever lied to you, sweetheart?"

She shook her head, but she was biting her lip again, a sure sign she was scared or nervous. "But Uncle Max, can I go by Mama and Mary?" she asked hopefully, glancing toward James who was bearing down on them quickly. "Please?" she asked, squeezing her eyes closed in a gesture that simply tore at his aching heart.

"Of course." He pointed across the room where Mary was getting her face painted and Sophie supervised. "Mama's right there." He waved when Sophie looked up. Their gazes met, collided, and silent messages and signals were sent. Max felt something warm and soft curl around his heart when Sophie and Mary waved toward him.

"See your mother, honey?" Max said. Carrie nodded, then waved to her sister. "Go on over there. Watch where you're going and watch all the people, honey. Okay? I'll stand right here and watch until you get to your mama. Okay?"

"Okay," Carrie said, darting another glance around him to see where Beardsley was.

"Okay, sweetheart. Go on. Your mother's waiting for you." Max watched as Carrie carefully scooted and dodged her way around the crowd of people and booths decorating the gym. When she got to her mother, Sophie waved to him to let him know Carrie was safe and with her.

"Max?" James called to him, waving his arm in the air and Max turned to the man, wondering what the hell he wanted. "Max McCallister," James called again as if they were long-lost buddies.

Max stayed where he was, rocking back on the heels of his boots. "What can I do for you?"

"I was wondering if you have a moment." James glanced around. "I'd like to speak to you."

"About what?" Max asked, crossing his arms across his chest.

"Well, perhaps we can go somewhere a bit more private."

One dark brow lifted and Max followed James's gaze which had followed and then landed on Sophie and the girls. Every protective instinct in him went on red alert.

"Perhaps not," Max snapped. "What's on your mind?" he demanded, causing James to shift uncomfortably, a small, rather annoyed smile still plastered on his face.

"Yes, well... I wanted to talk to you about Sophie," James began.

"What about her?" Max asked suspiciously, slipping his hands into his back pockets.

"I just wanted you to know that while I can appreciate you've been a major part of Sophie's and the girls' lives, my intentions toward Sophie are purely honorable."

"You don't say," Max said.

"Yes, absolutely," James confirmed with a nod of his head. "And while I know that Sophie has had a hard time of it since her husband passed away, I intend to make sure that she has everything and anything she needs in the future."

"And I assume you think what she needs is *you?*" Max asked in disbelief. How arrogant could this guy get? He didn't have a clue what Sophie wanted or needed.

James smiled, running a finger around the collar of his shirt. "Well, yes, if the truth be told. I mean, Max, come on now, you certainly can't expect Sophie to take someone like you seriously?"

"Excuse me?"

"I'm not blind. It's quite clear you have a...*thing* for Sophie," James said.

"A *thing?*" Max repeated.

"Yes, well, Max, I'm sure you can understand that Sophie is a wonderful woman—"

"That's the first thing you've said I agree with," Max snarled, realizing his temper was beginning to simmer.

"Max, we must be realistic here."

"Must we?"

"Yes." James hesitated. "I'm sure you can understand how awkward it might be to have Sophie's late husband's family continuing to insert themselves into our lives, especially once we're married."

"*Married?*"

"Yes. Married." James's face changed. "Oh dear. I'm so sorry, didn't you know?"

Max felt a slow fire ignite in his belly. "Are you telling me you and Sophie have discussed marriage?"

Sophie wouldn't lie to him, Max thought. She

wouldn't. In the ten years he'd known her, she had never willingly or knowingly deceived him and he wasn't about to believe she had now.

She'd told him she wasn't interested in getting married, nor was she even thinking about it.

But here James was telling him different.

The man had to be lying.

But still a ribbon of doubt and fear began to wind its way through Max, in spite of his attempts to push it back.

"Well, no," James admitted reluctantly and Max expelled a breath he hadn't known he'd been holding. "But I'm sure we will during our weekend away."

"You and Sophie are going away alone for a weekend?" Max asked.

"Why, yes. I thought a romantic weekend away might just be what the doctor ordered and with you here to stay with the children, it will be most convenient."

"Convenient?" Max repeated.

James hesitated, noting the look of disbelief on Max's face, then smiling again. "You don't believe me, do you?" He didn't wait for an answer. "Well, Max, if you don't believe me, ask Sophie. We just discussed our weekend away this afternoon in my office."

"You and Sophie talked about going away for the weekend just this afternoon?"

Sophie wouldn't lie to him, Max reasoned again. But she'd told him that she had only just begun dating this guy, so why on earth had she been discussing going away for the weekend with him? From what she'd told him, Max didn't think she knew Beardsley well enough to go anywhere alone with him, let alone a whole weekend.

So what the heck was going on?

He didn't know, but this certainly didn't sound like Sophie, at least not the Sophie he knew who had no hesitancy being honest and blunt regardless of the circumstances.

If she'd wanted him out of her life she certainly would have said something.

Wouldn't she?

Something akin to fear began to weave its way through Max, settling somewhere in his heart.

Sophie couldn't actually be serious about Beardsley, could she?

Then he remembered how defensive Sophie had been the night he'd confronted her about dating Beardsley, remembered, too, how uncomfortable she'd seemed.

He had surprised her by coming home. Maybe she hadn't been ready to discuss her relationship with this guy. Maybe she'd merely pacified him in order not to make waves his first night home.

And hadn't she questioned him about when he was leaving already?

Was it because she was anxious to have him out of her hair?

He didn't know, but he was damn sure going to find out.

He thought of Carrie and Mary, about the fear on little Carrie's face every time she even thought about Mr. Beardsley and something dark and dangerous began to stir in his gut.

"Yes, Max, we are going away for the weekend, as a matter of fact, in the morning I'll be rescheduling the date. While Sophie and I are taking this very slow, I have no doubt that eventually she'll realize that I'm the best man for her. And just between us I'm sure *you* can understand that your continued presence in Sophie's and the girls' lives might be just a tad bit awkward for all of us." Still smiling, James patted Max's arm. "I'm sure you can appreciate my position. After all, in the scheme of things I always believe it's best to start with a clean, organized slate without any messy issues of past relationships to cloud things up, don't you agree?"

"Beardsley, get a clue. You haven't said a thing I agree with," Max snarled, causing James to stiffen.

"Yes, well, I'm sorry you feel that way, Max. But suffice it to say that once Sophie and I are married I intend to clean up her life so to speak and get rid of all the hangers-on and the riffraff who are nothing but a drain on her time and emotions. I've waited a very long time to find the right woman, Max, and trust me, I'm not about to be derailed by some minor problems." He grinned. "Sophie and I *will* be married," he said confidently, absolutely certain of it.

"Hangers-on and riffraff?" Max repeated with a lift of his brow, knowing his temper was slipping away from him.

"Yes," James said firmly. "Feckless in-laws and irresponsible parents. Too many people have been cluttering up Sophie's life, preying on her kindness and her loyalty, taking advantage of her generous nature. She doesn't have the heart to tell these people that her life is in a different place now, a place where there's really no room for them, so to speak."

"No room for them?" Max repeated, stunned. "Are you saying Sophie's told you that there's no room in her life for me?"

"Oh, it's not just you, Max," James hedged. "But her mother as well. I mean, really. The woman is hardly a role model for children, not with her illustrious past, not to mention all those ridiculous relationships."

Max took a step closer, clenching his fists at his side so hard it hurt. "Watch it, buster. That's Sophie's mother you're talking about." He adored Carm and she certainly didn't deserve to be ridiculed or insulted by this jerk.

"Yes, she is Sophie's mother," James said with clear disdain. "But that doesn't automatically qualify her as a role model. Quite frankly, Max, Sophie's far too softhearted to say anything to these feckless, irresponsible hangers-on, so it will be up to me to take care of these matters.''

"Feckless, irresponsible hangers-on?" Max repeated. "I imagine that would be me?"

"I'm sorry, Max, but if the truth be told..." Splaying his hands, James gave Max a rueful smile. "As I said, I'm sure you understand."

"The only thing I truly understand," Max said as a misty red haze of anger wavered in front of his vision, blinding him to sense or reason. "Is that you're a complete and total idiot." Max took a step closer to James until the toes of his scuffed, scarred boots bumped up against James's perfectly polished wing tips. "Now, I've got something to say to you," Max said. "I'd be real careful about who you go around calling names and insulting. And that includes not just me, but Sophie's mother. I'd also be careful—*real* careful—about what you say to the twins and how you say it to them as well. Because if I were to find out that you yelled at Carrie or Mary or did anything at all to upset the girls or to scare them, or worse, if you did anything to make them *cry,* why James, I imagine I wouldn't be too happy, and you know what happens when the fecklessly irresponsible are unhappy." Max's eyes glittered dangerously.

"Are you threatening me with violence?" James asked, his voice catching on a tremble.

Smiling benevolently, Max slowly shook his head. "I'm not threatening you, James." Max pressed his nose right up against the smaller man's, making his face drain of all color. "I'm just saying that I would be extremely unhappy if you were ever to do any of those things to the girls. And you wouldn't want to do that." Max gave James one final, menacing look, then headed across the gym toward Sophie and the girls, leaving James stunned and staring openmouthed after him.

"Sophie." Spotting her, Max felt some of the tension ease out of him.

"What?" Alarmed by the look on his face, she reached for his arm. "What's wrong?"

"Nothing," he said. "Everything is just... wonderful." And he realized for the first time in his life, it was.

Chapter Seven

It ate at Max.

Everything Beardsley had said to him just kept echoing over and over in his mind, and as much as he tried to ignore it as the wistful whims of a desperate man, he wasn't quite so sure who the desperate man was. He needed time not only to think, but to talk to Sophie alone as well.

So Max merely bided his time, trying to figure things out.

That first weekend after the festival brought the first dusting of snow, but it was hardly more than flurries and melted as quickly as it fell.

By the second week in November, the temperature had dropped, settling in the upper teens or low twenties with more snow promised.

In the interim, Max continued to work like a madman on the basement playroom. He needed something to keep his hands and his mind occupied, something to keep his mind off what Beardsley had said, but no matter how hard he worked, his mind kept coming back to that conversation.

Part of the problem, he realized, was that his relationship with Sophie—and he didn't even know if that was the right word—was something that had never really been open and honestly discussed simply because of the circumstances.

When he and Michael had first met Sophie during college, Max realized immediately that Michael was also interested in Sophie. Knowing the kind of woman Sophie was, and what she wanted out of life, he realized that Sophie and Michael seemed to be much better suited than he and Sophie, simply because he'd been so involved in his budding career back then that he couldn't see giving it up to settle down and marry.

But Michael and Sophie had seemed to want the same things out of life, and he'd quickly realized he didn't fit into the picture—at least not her picture.

So, he'd buried the feelings that had hit him hard the very first time he'd laid eyes on her, buried them deep and stepped out of the way, leaving the path clear for his brother Michael while he set out to make his career.

And he had.

But he'd never told either of them how he really felt about Sophie, and perhaps that had been his first mistake.

He knew that Michael and Sophie had been having some trouble conceiving, but he'd had no idea how dire the situation or Michael's emotional health had become until they had come to him and asked him about the artificial insemination. It was at a time when he would have done anything to save his brother and his brother's marriage to Sophie. He'd had a responsibility to look after Michael, as he'd promised their parents before their deaths, and he'd done that.

But at whose expense, he wondered now.

Not that he regretted any of it, but was it wrong for him to want something for himself?

A home, a family, *his* children and the woman he'd always loved?

After Michael died, he thought then he'd have his chance with Sophie, but when he'd realized how devastated and grief-stricken she'd been, when he'd realized just how near the edge of collapse she was, he hadn't had the heart to dump this on her as well, fearing it might guarantee immediate rejection not just because she wasn't ready for it, but because she might think it was inappropriate. They had made an agreement never to discuss the twins' paternity, and he feared if he brought it up, when Sophie was already so devastated, it might just be too much for her.

So he hadn't said a word to Sophie about how he really felt about her or how he really felt about the girls or her raising them alone, deciding to give her some time.

He'd waited over ten years. What harm would a few more make, he'd reasoned?

And then Beardsley entered the picture, and as far as he was concerned all hell broke loose.

Perhaps the time had come to sit down and talk to Sophie, openly and honestly, and that included finding out exactly how she felt about him as well as Beardsley.

But he wasn't about to rush into this. He wanted to make sure that he chose a time and place where they were sure to have some privacy and at least several hours alone. Not an easy feat with twins in the house as well as another adult.

His chance came about three weeks after the Halloween festival and his infamous conversation with the Beardsley. Max was just putting the finishing touches on the basement playroom one evening when Sophie called down the stairs to tell him he had a phone call.

"Be right up," he called. He stopped on a step going up, glanced around and smiled. The playroom was done for all practical purposes. The mirror was being delivered and installed Friday afternoon—tomorrow, he realized with a frown. He'd been so physically and mentally occupied, the past few days had simply seemed to slip away from him, he thought as he continued up the stairs.

His other project, the carriage-house project as he'd been calling it, was also coming along nicely. The interior walls had already been torn down and rebuilt, while the plumbing, heating and electrical wiring had all been repaired or replaced. He'd made sure the workmen came during the day while Sophie was at school so she wouldn't see them and get curious. No point in planning a surprise if you couldn't keep it a surprise.

"Max?"

"Right here," he said, pushing open the basement door and grinning at the sight of her. Now that parent-teacher conferences were finally over, she wasn't quite so busy in the evenings. Now that the basement playroom was completed, he was hoping to spend more time with her. Like normal couples, he thought.

"You've got a call," she said, waving his cell phone at him.

He looked at her carefully, wondering why she seemed so tense and tight-lipped every time he got a call.

"Thanks." He took the phone from her, watching

as she pivoted and went right back into the living room. "Max McCallister," he said, leaning against the counter, then grinning. "Yeah, Sam, I'm fine. You're kidding? Starting when?" Max's brows drew together. "Next semester?" He laughed. "Uh, Sam, it's been a long time since I've been in school. When is the next semester? I mean when does it start? Third week in January?" Max thought about it for a moment. "Yeah, yeah, I think I can handle that. Send me the contracts. You've got the address here. Yeah, I'm sure, Sam, but thanks for asking. I'll talk to you soon. And as soon as that other thing comes through let me know. Okay, good night." With a satisfied sigh, Max flipped his cell phone closed and tried not to grin. Starting the third week in January, he, Max McCallister, was the newest professor in the Communications Department of the local community college. He wasn't going to tell Sophie yet, he thought. He wanted all of his ducks in a row before he made his pitch, and he still had a few ducks to line up. Shaking his head, Max grinned, delighted, then went in search of Sophie.

Sophie was standing in the living room, watching beautiful, fat flakes of snow drop lazily from the sky. The weatherman had predicted they might get as much as four inches tomorrow, but it looked like the snow was starting early.

Rubbing her hands up and down her arms, she

shivered as a cool draft floated in through the old windows.

Normally, she loved this time of the year, right before the holidays. The girls began to get so excited, first about Thanksgiving and then Christmas. With parent-teacher conferences finally over, she was able to spend more time with the girls, but this year there seemed to be an unbearable sadness hanging over her.

And she knew what it was: Max.

He'd been receiving phone calls on a regular basis the past few weeks. Not an evening went by that someone didn't call, and she'd been trying to prepare herself, trying to get her defenses up and trying to guard and protect her heart, knowing that the time was drawing near when Max would suddenly announce one evening that he was leaving. Again.

And this time, she thought, absently rubbing her heart, he was going to take her heart with him. She'd tried very hard these past few weeks to keep her emotions in check, but it had been futile and she knew it.

From that first night when Max had blown back into town, disrupting her life and making her nerves sing, she knew that she was sailing down a slippery slope when it came to Max and her heart.

From their first official date, through their many evenings together, to their jaunts and outings as a family with the girls, Sophie knew day by day she was losing the battle and losing her heart as well.

She'd come to depend on having Max around to lend a helping hand, not just with the girls, but with everything, including minor household chores. She no longer even thought about taking the garbage out twice a week simply because Max had taken that chore over. She no longer filled her car with gas because Max made sure it was always full. On Saturdays, she no longer had to do all the errands and chores herself. She and Max split them up, making everything go so much faster and lifting her load quite a bit.

She'd gotten so used to having him there, sharing everything in her day-to-day life she had no idea what she was going to do when he was gone.

Max had been home longer than usual this time, and although he'd spent a lot of his time building the playroom for the girls, he'd also spent just as much time *with* the girls, helping them with their homework, taking them to ballet class, going to the park with them, teaching them to ride their bikes.

The girls had come to depend on having Max in their life just as much as she had, and now simply took it for granted that Max would be there every day. They were going to be devastated when he left.

She'd tried to prepare them; she'd tried to talk to them, telling them that Uncle Max wouldn't be there forever, but her words seemed to fall on deaf ears.

The twins were positively convinced that this time Max was staying.

And she had no idea what to do about it.

Frustrated, Sophie shook her head. If she couldn't bear to face the reality of Max leaving, how on earth did she expect her children to?

She had no idea, nor had she any idea how she was going to manage without him, but she wasn't given a choice about such matters, in the same way she'd not been given a choice about so many things in her life.

So, she'd decided the only thing left for her to do was to allow herself and her daughters to enjoy Max while he was here, and worry about how she was going to cope with her own and the girls' disappointment later—after he'd left.

"Sophie? Are you all right?" Concerned, Max walked up behind her and placed his hands on her shoulders. Absently, she lifted a hand and covered his.

"I'm just watching the snow," she said quietly, turning her head to smile at him. Her eyes lit at the sight of him, drinking him in. "It's so peaceful and beautiful outside right now. Dark. Quiet." She let out a sigh. "Like there's no one else in the world." It certainly seemed that way, as if they were cocooned in a winter white wonderland.

"I know." Resting his chin atop her silky head, Max sighed as he looked out at the snow and slipped

his arms around her waist. "It's beautiful, Sophie."
He smiled. "It's been so long since I've been here
in winter I'd completely forgotten how wonderful
snow is."

She chuckled, leaning back against him, wanting
to feel his warmth. "Tell me that the next time we
have a blizzard."

"I just might," he said with a contented sigh.
"The playroom's done. Some time tomorrow afternoon the mirrors will be delivered and installed and
that should just about do it." He frowned. "Sophie,
are you worried at all about the girls falling against
the mirror and maybe getting hurt?"

Sophie smiled to herself. Max was extremely
overprotective about the girls, and it just warmed her
heart. Michael hadn't seemed to pay any attention
to them, not to their health or their welfare; his own
anger and resentment had robbed him of so much,
she thought sadly. As well as the girls.

And in her own way, she'd been responsible for
robbing Max of just as much, and it had been eating
away at her, she realized. She'd never considered
herself a selfish or inconsiderate person, but watching Max with the girls, watching the overwhelming
love and devotion he had to them, she'd begun to
feel guilty for all that she'd deprived him of. He
would have been a fabulous, loving, involved father.
And what more could a mother want for her
children?

"No, Max, I'm not worried." She turned her head to him with a smile. "The girls have been taking ballet classes for almost three years now, and they know the rules and the safety regulations. And if I'm not mistaken, don't all mirrors have to be shatterproof glass?"

"Yeah," he said with a little frown. "But I was just a little worried—"

"Max." She turned and wrapped her arms around his waist. "You're so sweet," she said softly. "Especially when it comes to the girls."

One brow rose. "And at other times, when it comes to other things?" he teased, making her shake her head and laugh. "I'm not so sweet, is that it?"

"Okay, Max, I'll confess you're always sweet."

"I don't think that's something men particularly strive for, Sophie. I mean, I can think of a lot better things a man might want to be other than sweet."

She chuckled again. "Yeah, well, don't tell that to a woman. Saying a man is sweet is about the ultimate compliment from a woman."

"So what about Beardsley?" he asked, unable to resist. "Do you think he's sweet?"

"James?" she said in surprise. "I don't know, I guess so." She thought about it for a moment. "Yeah, I guess James is sweet," she said, making Max scowl.

"Yeah, well, I've got a few other choice words for him and trust me, sweet isn't one of them."

"Max," she cautioned. "James is a very kind, nice man." His ridiculous offer to go away for the weekend notwithstanding, she thought.

Max was pretty sure he didn't like the idea of Sophie putting him and James in the same category. He was thoughtful for a moment. "Sophie, are you happy? I mean are you really happy?"

"You mean right now? At this very minute?" Her gaze met his and held. She had her arms around him, holding him close. He had his arms at her waist so she could feel his strength and warmth. It wasn't hard to figure out if she was happy. "Yeah, I guess I am happy," she admitted with a smile. "Especially at this particular moment," she added. He was here now, holding her, and the thought of him leaving was far away, so why wouldn't she be happy? "Why do you ask?"

He shrugged. "I don't know, the past couple of weeks you've seemed a bit down and distracted, and I was just wondering if something was bothering you."

If what Beardsley said was true, he imagined she was going to have to tell him sooner or later that she was going away with Beardsley and that Max was no longer going to be welcome in her life.

And quite frankly, he'd been dreading it, knowing he had no idea what he was going to do if she told him that. The only thing he knew was that he would never walk away from his children or abandon them.

Not ever.

The mere thought was enough to send him into a panic, and he knew he had to talk to her before she talked to him.

"I don't know that there's actually something bothering me," Sophie hedged, not wanting to admit that her case of the blues had more to do the fact that she knew Max would be leaving soon and she was powerless to prevent it. "I guess I've just had a lot on my mind the past few weeks. With the parent-teacher conferences, trying to get the girls ready for their ballet recital, get ready for Halloween and now Thanksgiving and soon Christmas. It's just been a little crazy around here. But then again it always is."

"True," he added with a smile. "But I hope I've been some help."

"Oh, Max." Instinctively, she lifted her hands to his chest. "Of course you've been a help. You've been a huge help. I don't know what I would have done without you the past few weeks, and certainly the girls wouldn't have a playroom if it wasn't for you. I'm very appreciative and grateful and if I've forgotten to tell you that, I'm sorry."

"No, no, you haven't," he said quietly. She was grateful and appreciative, and the thought simply annoyed him. The last thing he wanted was Sophie's gratitude.

"Max, I was waiting up for you to finish downstairs so I could remind you that you don't have to pick the girls up from school tomorrow.''

''I don't?'' he said with a lift of his brow, making her laugh and shake her head.

''No, Max, remember on Monday I explained the girls have a long weekend this weekend? They're off school tomorrow because we have a Teacher's Institute day, remember?''

''I seem to remember something...'' he said vaguely, letting his voice trail off.

''My mom's taking the girls downtown to see *The Nutcracker.*'' She ran her hands up and down her chilled arms, as he drew her closer to him, and farther away from the windows. ''It's an annual event for the three of them. They get up very early, take the train downtown, then they have lunch in a hotel, and go to the afternoon matinee. The girls love it. My mom also takes them window-shopping along Michigan Avenue after the ballet. By now, all the Christmas decorations are out and it's like a winter wonderland. By the time they come home tomorrow evening, they'll be so wound up and excited, they'll practically be out on their feet.''

''And this is a good thing, I guess?'' he said, not sounding too certain.

She laughed again. ''Absolutely. The girls love it and so does my mom. It's a very special tradition between them.''

"It's a shame you can't go," he said, drawing her even closer.

Her smile seemed sad. "Well, like I said, someone has to be the responsible one and I guess that's me."

"You know, Sophie, sometimes it wouldn't hurt to lean on someone else you know."

She glanced at his chest, then shook her head. "I tried that once, Max," she said quietly. "Remember? I depended on Michael and look at how that turned out." She smiled up at him. "Besides, Max, I've learned when a woman begins leaning on a man, if he decides to up and leave for whatever reason, it leaves a woman not just alone, but a little off balance. Once you've come to depend on someone, and they suddenly aren't there, it can be very painful for everyone involved." And she should know. That's exactly what had happened when Max had come home after Michael's death, and it was exactly what had happened now.

She'd ignored all her inner warnings and allowed herself to lean and depend on Max, and now, she knew that when he left it would be twice as painful. And lonely.

"Yeah, but Sophie, not all men are like Michael." He hesitated a moment. His loyalty to his brother was still strong, but his brother's behavior was inexcusable. "Sophie, I'm so sorry Michael disappointed you."

Surprised, she glanced up at him. They didn't really talk about Michael or her marriage very much. Max knew enough and had seen enough to know things had been bad, but she often wondered if he realized just how bad they'd really been.

"Max, it's not your fault," she said quietly. "Michael simply couldn't accept his own demons."

"That didn't give him a right to take it out on you and the girls though." Max frowned. "Especially the girls. They were simply helpless victims in all of this."

"I know," Sophie said with a sad sigh. "But fortunately they were still so young when Michael died they really don't remember how cold he'd been to them." She managed a smile, pushing her hair off her face. "And for that I'm grateful."

"Sophie, what time will your mom and the girls get home tomorrow?"

She smiled, realizing he was changing the subject. It always seemed that way. There were so many forbidden topics between them, so many things they could never comfortably talk about. Maybe someday they would be able to, she hoped.

"Oh, they won't be home probably until after dinner."

"Then why don't you and I go out for dinner? There's no point in cooking just for us. It's Friday anyway, a great way to start the weekend. Unless you've got other plans?"

She shook her head. "Nope, no other plans."

Relieved she wasn't going out with Beardsley, he grinned. "Then, what do you say?"

She nodded. "It's a date, Max, as long as I can wear comfortable clothes. I have an institute day tomorrow, so I'm not certain what time I'll get home."

"Well, does that mean it's usually before or after the regular time?"

She shrugged. "It depends how the meetings go. How about if I call you from school when I'm getting ready to leave?"

"Great. Then I can pick you up."

"Only if you drive me to school in the morning as well, otherwise I'll have to leave my car in the school parking lot overnight and I don't really want to do that since it's Friday. And leaving my car in the lot is simply an invitation to trouble."

"Fine. I'll drive you to school in the morning."

"You're sure?"

"Positive."

Stifling a yawn, Sophie covered her mouth, then shook her head. She was far more tired than she'd realized, but every night while Max had been working in the basement, she'd been staying up waiting for him to finish so they could spend some time together. "It's late. I'd better get to bed. I have to get up early."

"Okay," he said, but made no move to let her go.

"Max?" Lifting her chin, she met his gaze. "Is something wrong?"

"No, Sophie. As a matter of fact, hopefully in a few days everything will be just right." Unbearably aroused just by her nearness, he drew her closer.

"Max." Her fingers curled into his shirt as she cautiously tried to step back. She wasn't going to help herself or her heart if she didn't stop getting drawn into him and the enormous, wonderful feelings he evoked in her.

"Sophie." He lowered his head, took her mouth before she could protest or push him away. It had been too long since he'd touched her, held her, kissed her. Even though he'd made a habit of kissing and touching her every single day if he could, it still wasn't enough. He wanted more than just stolen kisses and touches. He wanted everything. He wanted Sophie.

Clinging to his shirt, Sophie moaned softly, the snow and the chilly wind forgotten as heat swept through her, blinding her to everything but the sensations sweeping through her body.

Pressing herself closer to Max, she could feel his masculine hardness pressing against her and it filled her with an unbearable longing. She lifted her hands to his shoulders, gripping them tightly, rising on tiptoe to meet the passion pouring out of him.

Unconsciously, she tugged at his shirt, wanting to feel the warmth of his bare skin under her hands, groaning softly when the old shirt all but gave under her hands.

Max groaned as she pressed against him, urging him higher, making his brain pool into a puddle of mush until he couldn't think, but only feel the intense heat of lust, desire and passion, burning through him like a wildfire, threatening to flare out of control.

His hands molded to her slender, curved hips, pulling her closer until they were nearly fused together, body to body, clinging to one another in a burst of need and desire that recklessly pushed him almost past the point of control.

Regretfully, he dragged his mouth from hers, cursing himself and the fact that he couldn't do this. Not now. Not here. Not like this. He hadn't waited patiently all this time to take Sophie like some careless, randy teenager.

He respected her too much.

For her, he wanted everything to be perfect.

"Well." It never failed to astound her the way her body responded to Max. "I'd better say goodnight." She stepped out of his arms and headed toward the steps on shaky legs. She glanced out the window at the still-falling snow. "Hopefully we won't get more than the four inches the weatherman predicted."

"Hey, I'd love a good old-fashioned snowstorm, I've been in the desert, remember?"

"I remember, Max," she responded with a laugh. "But only someone who hasn't been in a real snowstorm for a while can say that." She lifted her hand. "Good night, Max."

"'Night, Sophie." He stood there for a long time after she'd gone upstairs, knowing that tomorrow during dinner he was finally going to plead his case. The girls deserved a father, and who better than their real one?

By tomorrow night, Sophie MacCallister and his daughters would finally be his.

"Max," Sophie said early the next morning as she squinted and tried to see out the windshield, even though he was driving. "I think the weatherman lied," she said with a frown as she peered at the heavy flakes of snow that were still falling.

Four inches had been predicted, but right now they'd already had at least eight inches overnight with no promise of it stopping anytime soon, and it was barely eight in the morning.

"No kidding," Max said, gripping the wheel tighter as he inched along the street. Thankfully Sophie only lived about five blocks from school so he didn't have far to go. "I hope your mom and the girls got downtown all right."

Sophie smiled. "I'm sure they did. They left so

early this morning, before six, that I'm sure they beat the heaviest snow down there.''

''I hope so.'' Max scowled as he tried to steer around a slippery corner and found himself fishtailing. Concentrating, he quickly brought the car under control. He may not have driven in a winter snowstorm in many years, but once you learned how to drive in the snow you never forgot it. ''Sophie, what happens if this keeps up? I mean will the trains still run? Will your mom and the girls be able to get home?''

''I'm not sure, Max. I guess it depends on how much accumulation we actually get and when the snow finally stops.'' She patted his arm. ''But don't worry. If worse comes to worst my mom and the girls will stay in a hotel overnight.''

''Have they ever done that before?'' he asked worriedly.

Sophie chuckled. ''Yes, Max, if you live in the Midwest, everyone knows this time of year you really do have to be prepared for anything. It's called a backup plan.'' She peered out the window again. ''With any luck James will let us go home early today.''

''James is going to be there?'' he asked in a tone of voice that had her sighing.

''Max, he's the vice principal of the school. Of course he's going to be there. He's one of the coordinators in charge of the day.''

"Terrific," Max muttered, making Sophie laugh.

"I guess when you told me you didn't like him, you meant it?" She turned to him. "And I gather you haven't changed your mind since?"

He gave her a mild look. "No, I haven't changed my mind." His jaw set as he flipped his directional on to pull in front of the school. "I don't like the guy and I don't trust him," he said firmly. "Nor do I like the idea of him wooing you."

One brow lifted. "But it's okay for you to woo me?" she teased, remembering what Max had said to her on their official date.

"Yeah. Hell yeah," he said firmly as he brought the car to a stop right in front of the double doors Sophie had to go in. He noted she didn't deny that James had been wooing her.

Laughing, Sophie shook her head, then leaned over to kiss his cheek. "You're incorrigible, Max."

He turned his head toward her just as her lips grazed his cheek, catching her mouth with the corner of his own. He lifted a hand to the back of her head, holding her close, drawing her deeper into the kiss.

"Max." Self-consciously, Sophie pushed against his chest, embarrassed to be kissing Max in front of the school. "Let's not get me fired for conduct unbecoming a teacher."

"Do they have those kinds of rules?" he asked with a frown.

"I don't know," she admitted with a laugh. "But

I'd prefer not to find out.'' She opened the door, grateful she'd worn heavy wool slacks and a heavy sweater and her winter boots. The snow was past her ankles since the plows hadn't gotten to the circular drive that fronted the school. Since there was no school today it wasn't necessary to get this section done immediately. "I'll call you when I'm ready to leave.''

"Okay. Have a good day.''

She smiled. "You, too, Max. You, too.''

Max had planned to make reservations somewhere that wasn't too fancy or wouldn't require Sophie to have to dress up, but by noon the snow hadn't stopped and the weather reports were predicting an accumulation of up to twenty additional inches.

He had a feeling they weren't going anywhere tonight and headed toward the nearby grocery store on foot, grateful for the first time that when Sophie and Michael had gone shopping for a house, she'd insisted it be within walking distance to work, a major grocery store, banks and other amenities necessary to suburban life, because there was no way he could get either his car or hers dug out.

And certainly not with one arm. While his shoulder had almost healed, the past few weeks while he'd been working on the playroom, he hadn't exactly babied it, and now it was still sore and aching, so trying to shovel out wasn't an option.

When he returned from the grocery store, which was all but deserted, he was frozen from the blowing snow and wind. Fearing he might have missed Sophie's call, he immediately played the two messages that had come in while he was gone.

The first call was from the company he'd purchased the mirror from, telling him they were canceling delivery today because of the weather.

"No kidding," Max muttered, pressing Play again to hear the second message. Carm's cheerful voice spilled into the room.

"Sophie dear, it's Mom. The ballet has been canceled due to inclement weather, so the girls and I are just going to stay downtown tonight. We've gotten a room and plan on ordering room service and watching movies until the weather clears. I'll leave my cell phone on if you need to reach us, but never fear, darling, all is well and we're having a ball." Carm chuckled. "I hope you and Max have as much fun being snowbound as we plan on doing. *Ciao,* darling."

Grinning, Max couldn't help but feel his spirits soar. If Carm and the girls were going to be downtown all night, that meant he and Sophie would be alone.

All night.

Wanting everything to be perfect, Max unpacked

his bag of groceries. He'd gotten a bouquet of fresh flowers, a bottle of excellent white wine, two filets and two very large Idaho potatoes to bake, along with some lettuce to make a salad. While he was far from a cook, not even close, even he could manage to cook a steak and bake a potato.

He hoped.

He set the table up in the living room, laid the firewood so they could have a fire, placed Sophie's flowers in a vase it took him nearly half an hour to unearth, and then set out every candle he could find, wanting to set a calm, quiet romantic mood.

He took a shower and changed out of his cold, damp clothes. When he came back downstairs it was almost three in the afternoon and Sophie still hadn't called and the snow hadn't stopped.

Frowning, he went to the front window. The snow was still coming down with blazing speed, creating a near white-out condition where visibility was relatively zero.

Pacing the floors, Max waited, wondering why on earth Beardsley didn't let the teachers go early today. Couldn't the man see they were in the middle of a blizzard and the later it got the more dangerous driving on the roads would be.

With nothing really left to do until Sophie called, Max stretched out on the couch to watch the news. Within minutes, he was asleep.

When the phone finally rang at four-thirty, it startled him awake. Blinking, he realized it was dark outside already. Unfolding himself off the couch, he shivered, wondering why it was so cold in the house.

When he went to turn on the lamp, nothing happened. He glanced at the television. It, too, was black. They must have lost power sometime while he was napping.

No power meant no food, he thought with a frown as he grabbed up the telephone.

"Sophie?" he said without preamble.

"Yeah, it's me," she said, sounding weary and tired. "I'm done. Finally."

"All right, it may take me a little while to get there but just wait for me right in front where I dropped you off."

"Max, please, drive carefully. I understand it's awful out there." She hesitated. "Max, listen, I know we're supposed to have a date tonight, but it's miserable out. And I'm worried about you driving. James has offered to take me to his house until it stops snowing. He only lives about two blocks away and we could walk if we had to."

Max's fingers tightened on the receiver. "That's not necessary, Sophie," he said easily. "I'll be there in a jiffy."

"Max, are you sure?" she asked worriedly. "It's dangerous to be driving."

He grinned. "Don't worry, I promise I'll be safe, if not slow. Just wait for me right in front of where

I dropped you off this morning.'' Hanging up the receiver, Max grabbed his coat, gloves and his house keys, then snatched the afghan off the couch before making his way down the back steps and out the door.

Come hell or high water he was going to pick up Sophie. He wasn't about to let her go home with Beardsley. He didn't trust that fool as far as he could throw him.

Shutting and locking the back door behind him, Max mucked his way through the snow, ducking his head against the wind and hunching his shoulders as he made his way toward the garage.

He might not be able to get either of their cars dug out, but he wasn't going to let a little thing like no transportation stop him.

He shoved the side door to the garage open and stepped inside out of the snow which had stung his cheeks, soaked his boots and settled wetly in his hair. With a sigh of relief, he saw the girls' sled hanging on the wall and headed toward it.

''Sophie, hold my hand so you don't fall. The power's out and there's no lights,'' Max said, reaching for her hand as he led the way back into the dark house.

''I still cannot believe you came to get me with a sled,'' she said with a chuckle of amazement. It had to be the most romantic thing a man had ever done for her.

She felt like a princess in one of those fairy tales when Max had walked up to school, battling the wind and snow, pulling the sled behind him like a knight in shining armor coming to rescue the trapped princess. He'd bundled her onto the sled, covered her with the afghan, then began trudging through the almost knee-deep snow, lugging the sled and her behind him all the way home.

"Hey, beggars can't be choosers," he said, climbing the back stairs and clutching her hand tightly in his. "Do you have any flashlights in the house?"

"Third drawer on the right in the cabinet next to the refrigerator."

"Thank God you're a reliable creature of habit," he said, as he let go of her hand to move to the cabinet, fumbling around until he found two flashlights. He turned them both on and then handed her one.

"Here. You're going to have to get into some warm, dry clothing, Sophie, you're soaked. And frozen," he added, brushing snow out her dark hair.

"So are you," she said, shining the flashlight on him and grinning. "I still cannot believe you thought of the sled." Shaking her head and dislodging some wet, heavy snow, she chuckled again. "I wish you could have seen James's face. It was priceless."

"Yes, I'm sure he was impressed," Max commented, not bothering to conceal his disdain. "Now, Sophie, go upstairs and take a hot shower so you don't catch cold. I don't know that the water will be hot without power, but it might still be warm. Put something warm and heavy on while I get things started down here. I'll get our dinner started."

"Dinner?" she repeated in surprise. "Max, if we don't have any power, we can't cook anything."

One brow lifted in challenge. "Want to bet? One thing my job has taught me is how to be resourceful, Sophie, and trust me, we're going to eat dinner tonight."

Too tired to argue with him, she shrugged. "Okay, fine. I'll go take my shower."

"Let me walk you to the steps." He took her hand, and using his flashlight, he led the way out of the kitchen, through the dining room and into the living room. His flashlight beam caught just the edge of the set table and the bouquet of flowers and wine sitting atop it.

"Oh, Max." Sophie's gaze flew to his. "I can't believe you went to so much trouble and now everything's ruined."

"No, it's not," he countered, still holding on to her as he led her toward the steps. "Everything's going to be just fine." He pressed a soft, quick kiss to her lips. "Trust me, now. I wouldn't lie to you."

"Okay," she said dubiously, shivering a bit as

she used her own flashlight to light her way as she slowly and carefully climbed the steps. ''I'll be down in a few minutes.''

''Terrific.'' Max grinned at her retreating back, holding his flashlight just above her so she could see the steps better. ''Then we'll begin tonight's adventure.''

Chapter Eight

"Max, if I didn't know better I'd swear you were a Boy Scout," Sophie said with a chuckle, leaning back against the couch in the living room and sipping her wine. Candles were lit and scattered throughout the room and a fire blazed brilliantly in the hearth.

"Sorry, Sophie, but group homes or foster homes don't exactly allow for such niceties as the Boy Scouts," he said, stoking the fire once before scooting back to sit next to her and lean against the couch. He pulled the comforter over their legs to keep them warm. Even though the power and the heat were still off, with the fire and the blankets and comforters they were warm.

"So how on earth did you learn how to be so resourceful?" she asked curiously. Whenever Max talked about his childhood, he did so without any trace of anger and bitterness, and it always amazed her since she couldn't help but feel sadness that he and Michael hadn't had the benefit of a loving family growing up. She couldn't help but wonder how much that contributed to the way the two brothers had grown up.

"When you've lived alone for thirty-five years and in all the remote places of the world I have, you learn to be resourceful or you starve, or in some cases, worse," he added softly, sipping his own wine.

"Well, all I have to say is thank goodness you are so resourceful or we wouldn't have eaten tonight." With a contented sigh, Sophie laid her head on his shoulder.

They'd had baked potatoes cooked right in the glowing wood at the base of the fire, and grilled filets. Max had taken one of the oven grates and set it right atop the blazing fire, using it as a grill and setting the steaks on it to cook. She'd put together a salad and they'd had a fabulous dinner.

Now, fed, warm and content, Sophie simply allowed herself to relax. It had been so long since she'd had just a simple, quiet evening to herself without homework, baths, bedtime snacks and glasses of water, to say nothing of preparing herself for the next work day that she expected to take full advantage of this evening.

"Did you have a good day?" Max asked, slipping his arm around her to cradle her closer. He liked having her lean against him. Liked feeling her soft, womanly curves pressed against him.

She chuckled, sipped her wine. "I don't know if you'd call it a good day. It was a lot of sitting around listening to a bunch of administrators blather away." She snuggled closer. "To tell you the truth, I was so concerned about the weather and whether or not I was going to be able to get home, I wasn't paying much attention."

Lazily, he began to stroke his hand over her shoulder, occasionally brushing the bare skin of her collarbone. Her pulse increased and a shudder raced over her.

After her shower, she'd put on a thick terry-cloth robe, the heaviest and warmest one she had, but right now, she was sorry it was so thick and heavy. Right now, content, full and terribly relaxed, she ached to feel the touch of Max's fingers on her bare skin.

Shaken, she sipped her wine again.

"It seems so quiet without the girls," Max said a bit wistfully, still absently caressing her shoulder. "I don't think we've ever been alone before. At least not totally alone."

"I know," she said with a long, slow sigh. "As

much as some days and nights I want nothing more than a few minutes of peace and quiet, when the girls are gone overnight like this, the quiet in the house drives me crazy."

He grinned. "You miss them?"

She nodded, laughed. "Always," she admitted. "Even some days at school I get this sharp pang of just wanting or needing to see them." Her smile bloomed as it always did when she talked about the girls. "I never realized how happy two little girls could make me."

"I know, Sophie," he said quietly. "I never realized the joy or the hold kids could have on you, either," he said, realizing he was treading on sacred ground here, and wondering if he should continue. "And you're a terrific mother," he added when she didn't say anything to encourage him to go on. "The best."

Self-consciously Sophie glanced down at her wine. "Well, I've tried, Max." She shrugged. "I just do the best I can and hope for the best."

He glanced at the fire for a moment, not quite certain how to start this. "Sophie, can we talk about something?"

His voice was so serious she turned to look at him. "Of course, Max, we can talk about anything." The look on his face made her spirits drop. "Don't tell me you want to talk about James again?" she all but groaned. The last thing she wanted to do on this one quiet evening alone with Max was talk about James.

The truth of the matter was she was terribly embarrassed about the whole thing. She'd agreed to date James as an experiment, a way to get her back out in the world, socializing. But apparently James's idea of dating and taking it slow wasn't exactly the same as hers. And after all the grief Max had given her before about dating James, she wasn't about to admit to Max she'd made a mistake in judgment about James, something she hadn't truly realized until now.

He was a very nice man, and she was certain he would make someone a wonderful beau, friend and husband. But not her. Definitely not her.

Not to anyone, especially Max would she admit that when she'd realized the girls didn't like him, and that he'd yelled at her daughters, that had all but sealed James's fate. She would never allow anyone to mistreat her babies. Not anyone.

But having to admit to Max that once again she'd made a mistake in judgment about a man would be far too embarrassing.

She should have known better. But she hadn't and didn't, Sophie thought with a weary sigh, simply because she'd had so little experience with men, and if the truth be told, she wasn't all that anxious to have a relationship with a man.

Except for Max.

The one man in the world who was definitely off-limits.

"You don't want to talk about James?" he said, turning to her and trying to hide his disappointment. His gaze met hers, held, and Sophie's pulse began to thud recklessly.

"No, Max, I don't," she said quietly. She licked her suddenly dry lips as his fingers continued to caress her shoulder, slipping down to her bare neck and collarbone, sending fingers of delightful shivers racing up and down her back.

Still caressing her, her sweet scent rose up to intoxicate and seduce, making him long. Max's gaze locked on hers. "What would you like to talk about, Sophie?" he asked, his voice so quiet in the darkened room it was almost a whisper.

Her heartbeat began to quicken at the look in his eyes. It was the same look he'd had the night they'd gone to dinner downtown, a look that made her feel beautiful, desirable, wanted.

It was a look she'd never seen in a man's eyes before and she relished it. That look, she thought hazily, made her want and yearn for all the things she knew she couldn't have, not forever at least. And she'd always known she was a forever kind of woman, and some things never changed. She couldn't and wouldn't settle for less.

But maybe, just maybe she could have those

things, all those wonderful glorious things just for one night—just for tonight.

Max was here now, and she'd promised herself she'd enjoy him while he was here.

Was it so wrong? she wondered. To want just one simple night for herself? To give in to the feelings and emotions, needs and desires that she'd kept hidden and buried for so long. A night of wonderful memories to savor and treasure during all the long, lonely nights after he was gone?

At the moment, she was weary and tired, and wanted only to lose herself in Max's arms, and not worry about tomorrow or the future, only think about this moment.

She'd never been a brave woman; she'd always known that about herself. If she had been brave, she would have gone after what she really wanted years ago—Max.

Maybe she couldn't have him forever, but she could have him for tonight, and that, she decided, would have to be enough.

"I don't want to talk, Max," she said, setting her wineglass down on the floor and turning to him. "I want to kiss you."

He smiled, a slow, lazy smile that sent her pulse and her heart scrambling. She couldn't wait. She leaned forward, braced his face in her hands and began raining kisses all over him, soft, gentle kisses meant to both comfort and arouse.

His breath hitched, and then his arms clamped down tightly around her, dragging her close and all but on top of him as he crushed his mouth to hers, murmuring her name over and over again.

"Sophie. Sophie. Sophie." When he slid down to the floor, she went with him. When he slipped his fingers under the collar of her robe and pushed it off her shoulders to plant a ribbon of kisses on her bare skin she shuddered, closed her eyes, clutched him close and gloried in the feelings that were building like a volcano.

Arching her back, she pressed closer to him, wanting to feel his entire body, his skin, his touch.

Her fingers dragged at his shirt, pulled it out of his jeans, then slid under the material to roam his wide, broad back, absently fingering an old scar, marveling at how warm and strong he was.

Half-mad and breathless, Max pushed her robe off her shoulders, reveling in the sight and scent of her beautiful, naked skin. He started kissing her from the soft column of her throat, sweetly making his way down her body, causing soft little gasps to escape her.

"Max." Frantic, she tugged at his jeans, wanting, needing to feel him, bare skin to bare skin as he pushed open her robe entirely and simply lifted his head to look at her.

"Sophie. You are the most beautiful thing ever

created." His words, soft as a whisper, as reverent as a prayer caused her eyes to sting with tears.

"Max. Oh, Max." Clinging to him, she sipped at his mouth, their tongues playing, teasing, touching.

With a moan, he tore his mouth from hers, raining kisses down skin. He inhaled deeply of her scent, wanting to drown himself in it, in her.

She moaned softly, digging her nails in his back as his mouth gently brushed against her nipple, causing it to pucker then pout. She arched upward, wanting, needing more as the fire of desire blazed higher, hotter, almost making her cry out with frustration and need.

Her hands ran the length of his back, up and down, but she wanted more. Needed more. Years of pent-up desire and yearning for him had made her frantic, greedy, and she shoved at his jeans, wanting no barriers between them. Not anymore.

He groaned softly, lifting himself as she pushed down his jeans and reached for him. He struggled for breath, for control, but knew it was useless. He'd waited and wanted her for too many years to control himself now.

Clinging to one another, breaths mingling, hearts soaring, they thrashed and rolled over the comforter, unaware of the hard floor beneath them, ignoring the chill in the air. The heat between them was more than enough to warm their bodies, their lonely, aching hearts.

He cradled her face in his hands, pushing her hair gently off her face so he could see her. He needed to see her now, at the moment she became his.

Only his.

He'd waited so long that now, he could wait no longer.

He angled himself over her, struggling to hold back his desire, stronger now than at any moment in his life, any moment in memory.

"Sophie." He said only her name, but felt her arms come around him, enclose him, welcome him as she drew him down, and into her, giving herself to him, all of herself and all that she was.

She moaned softly at the first slick entry, wiggling her body to adjust to his hard, masculine weight.

His eyes all but rolled back in his head at the pleasure, enormous, intense and so long awaited. She was his dream, his life, all that he'd ever wanted—the symbol of all the things, the good things he could never have.

Driven higher by need, by desire so strong it felt as if his heart was going to thud out of his chest, Max held his breath, tried to slow himself down, but like a runaway freight, his body had a mind of its own.

Moaning softly, Sophie dug her teeth into his shoulder. The pleasure was so great, so strong, so full of life and energy, she'd never felt anything like it.

It was as though a whirlwind had picked her up and was still tossing her about, leaving her breathless and full of wonder at the beauty that flowed, sparked and meshed between them.

They were finally joined, hearts, minds and bodies as one, as they'd both wanted and desired, but had deprived themselves for reasons that now were too elusive to recall.

Nothing this glorious, this miraculous could be wrong, Sophie thought as the storm tossed her higher and she moved with Max, her body arching and moving to meet his every move, his every thrust.

She continued to cling to him, pressing her mouth to any part of him she could reach, wanted to inhale him and his essence, to imprint this moment and him in her memory.

She cried out as he pressed higher, drove them both higher. Max clung to her, his breath panting out of him like a dying man, his nerves screaming and singing for relief.

His hands gripped her slender hips. So delicate, he thought hazily, so soft, so feminine. He lifted her, drove in deeper, harder, faster until they were both gasping, breathless and ready to die of pleasure.

"Max. Oh, Max." She dug her heels in, feeling as if she was flying off the ends of the earth. Then her eyes slammed shut as the whirlwind of pleasure ruthlessly grabbed her and tossed her up and over the edge, making her cry out against his mouth, buck against his body.

"Sophie." His name burst out of her as everything inside of him exploded in a frantic rush of heated passion as he followed her over the blissful edge and into sweet oblivion.

"Well." Sophie finally managed to say after long, silent moments cradled quietly in Max's arms. The fire still blazed bright and golden hot, but the candles had nearly burned down, leaving the living room in hazy shadows.

"Is that a good 'well' or a bad 'well'?" he asked, looking up at her face and sliding off her.

"Definitely a 'wowie-kazowie wow,'" she assured him with a smile as he cuddled next to her. More than content, Sophie slid her arms around him, not wanting to let him go.

"Yeah, I'd have to agree." Comfortable, he laid his head on her chest and waited for his breathing and heart to regulate. "It's a good thing I don't have a heart condition," he murmured, bending his head to nuzzle her.

A shiver raced over her and the fire of need began stirring once again in her belly. She'd never felt this unbearable, uncontrollable torrent of need before. Nor had desire ever stoked so hot so fast or left her so shaken. She'd never wanted a man so much, nor had she ever wanted one again so soon after making love with him.

"Why?" she asked, tenderly brushing his dark hair off his face. "Why is it a good thing you don't have a heart condition?"

"Because I think you would have killed me, Sophie," he admitted with a chuckle, still nuzzling her.

She gave him an affectionate pinch, trying to ignore what his clever little mouth was doing to her already overloaded system. "Is that a complaint?"

He sighed in contentment, more at peace than he'd ever been in his life. "Sophie, that's a supreme compliment."

"Good." Shifting her weight to get closer to him and more comfortable, she glanced around. "I wonder what time it is?"

"Why?" he asked with a mischievous grin. "Going somewhere?" His hand absently began stroking over her hip, tracing delicious little circles, then sliding down to tease the tender skin of her thigh.

"Not at the moment." She glanced up at him with a wicked smile. "Except maybe to bed," she teased, doing a little stroking and nibbling of her own.

"Are you uncomfortable?" he asked worriedly, realizing they were still lying on the hard floor, on a comforter, but it was still hard. "Did I hurt you?"

"Max." She lifted her hand to his cheek, then kissed him gently. "Don't worry about me. I'm not hurt. It's not uncomfortable and I'm perfectly fine."

She chuckled, kissing him again. "Actually more than fine."

"Yeah?" He grinned.

"Yeah," she said with a grin of her own. He had the most tantalizing mouth, she thought hazily, pressing her lips to his again. "I love kissing you. Did you know that?" she murmured, teasing his mouth with hers until he was moaning softly in his throat and reaching for her.

"You do?" he replied, and she nodded.

"You taste wonderful," she murmured with a lusty sigh as she slid on top of him.

"Wonderful, huh?" he murmured as desire wound its way through him again. He shifted her hips, lifted her until she was sitting atop him.

His breath caught and he was pretty sure his eyes had just crossed. Slowly, she began to move, the look of a contented, satisfied cat on her face.

"Uh…Sophie…are you sure you're up to this?" he managed to ask, letting his eyes slide closed as pleasure grabbed at him with slick, greedy fingers.

"The question is, are *you* up to it, Max?" she asked as she moved a bit faster, watching his mouth go slack and his eyes glaze as passion greedily grabbed him again, snaring him in its grasp.

"Sophie." His body quivered, his heart gave one long, slow lurch as he struggled to maintain at least some modicum of control.

"Well, Max," she purred, running her fingers

through the thick patch of hair on his chest. Back and forth, lightly, gently trailing over his nipples, making him groan and arch toward her. She held herself off him a bit, lovingly teasing and tormenting him. "Are you up to it?"

She laughed when he groaned softly, then finally dug his fingers into her hip for purchase, and pulled her down fully atop him. Another groan escaped him as they began to move, riding together toward oblivion.

His eyes slid closed in pleasure, the last sight, the last thought that filled his heart was Sophie.

The lights were on. Max woke up in Sophie's bed, squinting when he realized sometime during the night the power had come back on. Lights blazed throughout the house, and heat filled the air. It was still chilly from the lack of heat for so many hours and would probably take several hours to finally warm up, but he figured he and Sophie had kept each other plenty warm enough.

He glanced at her, sleeping quietly beside him. Her dark hair was tousled in her face. One arm was flung over her head, and her mouth was perched in a half smile.

He figured they'd maybe gotten two hours of sleep. The rest of the time they'd simply greedily devoured one another, unable to get enough, unable to satisfy the yearning that had been building for so many years.

Sliding out of bed naked, Max realized his body was sore and achy. It had been a long time since he'd made love on a hard floor, probably not since he was a teenager, but that hadn't dampened the experience any.

He padded to the window and glanced out, pleased that the snow had finally stopped. Giving one more quick glance at Sophie to make sure she was still sleeping, he put on a pair of jeans, then slipped out of the room and headed downstairs to make some coffee.

If ever there was a morning for coffee this was it, he thought, dragging a hand through his hair and pushing it off his face before stifling a huge yawn.

He almost groaned when he caught sight of the living room. The fire had burned out and was now simply cold embers of white ash. The flue was still open and he could feel the rush of outside cold air rush in. Shivering, he went to the fireplace and closed the flue, rubbing his hands up and down his arms.

He grabbed the comforters they'd left sprawled on the floor and quickly folded them and put them on the couch. The candles from last night had all burned down. Now, he gathered them and carried them with him into the kitchen to toss in the trash.

Morning sunlight bright as a diamond and as brilliant as a rainbow shone through the kitchen windows, making him wince at the brightness.

Padding to the trash, he tossed the used candles, then reached for the coffeepot. Fortunately, he'd been here long enough to know where everything was kept, and he made short work of brewing a pot of coffee, leaning against the cabinet, staring outside, waiting for the coffee to finish. He had no idea what time it was. All the clocks had stopped yesterday when the power was off, and he'd left his watch upstairs on Sophie's nightstand.

Last night had been incredible, he decided. That was the only word for it. Incredible and unbelievable. It was funny, he'd had fantasies about making love to Sophie for years, but he'd never even imagined it would be as good as it had been.

Still thinking about last night, Max grabbed two mugs from the cabinet and filled one with coffee, sipping slowly and savoring the fragrant brew.

With his cup still in his hand, he opened the refrigerator. Although the power had been off for probably a good sixteen hours, the refrigerator hadn't been opened in all that time, so he imagined that all the food was still good.

He hoped.

He reached for the carton of eggs and the package of bacon. Both were still chilled, if not icy cold, he thought as he dragged out a couple of frying pans and began to prepare breakfast.

* * *

Sophie was still sound asleep when he carried their breakfast tray upstairs. He set it down on the nightstand, then sat on the edge of the bed.

She looked so calm and peaceful, he thought wistfully, stroking a hand down her bare back. She groaned softly, then shifted, muttering something under her breath.

Grinning, he leaned down and began planting a necklace of kisses across her neck and down her back. She moaned, shifted, then lifted her head, shoving her hair out of her face.

"Are we still alive?" she mumbled, looking at him bleary-eyed and making him laugh.

"Just barely, I think," he answered, kissing her on the lips. She kissed him back, then scowled.

"What time is it?" She sat up, dragging the sheet with her to cover herself. It was ridiculous to feel modest after the night they'd had, but still, she did. She sniffed suspiciously. "Is that coffee?" Eyes narrowed, she sniffed again, then sat up fully. "Give it," she ordered, extending a hand toward the steaming mug sitting on the tray.

"Careful, it's hot," he cautioned, carefully handing her the mug.

She sipped the steaming brew, letting the caffeine blast through her system. "Ahh, a man who can make decent coffee is definitely a man after my own heart," she muttered, closing her eyes in satisfaction.

"Uh, you've got that right, Sophie. I'm definitely a man after your heart."

Her eyes opened suspiciously as she put both hands around her mug to steady it and continued to sip. "What do you mean?"

He grinned at her. "Just what I said, Sophie, I'm a man after your heart." He shrugged, figuring there was no time like the present. He pressed a kiss to her shoulder. "I don't want you thinking I'm just after your body."

A faint warning was beginning to hum in her brain and that suspicious tickle was starting at the back of her neck. Again.

"Max, I'll admit last night was wonderful. Incredible. Unbelievable." With a laugh, she shook her head, still unable to believe what they had between them. It was miraculous. That was the only word she could think of. Now, she finally understood the power of lovemaking when you loved someone. And that was the key, she knew, she was wildly and hopelessly in love with Max and had been for so long she couldn't even remember when it had happened. She'd loved Michael but now she knew she'd never been 'in love,' not until Max.

"But you're making me nervous here, Max," she admitted. "Could you please just tell me what you're saying? I'm not very good at playing word games.''

"I'm not either, Sophie." He locked his gaze on hers. "Sophie, I want you to marry me."

Stunned, she looked at him, not wanting to get her hopes up. She had a feeling there was a lot more to Max's question than he was letting on. "Why?" she asked.

"Why what?" he asked with a frown.

"Why on earth do you want to marry me?" Sophie held her breath. She'd never expected a marriage proposal from Max. "Not a month ago you told me pigs would fly before you got married," she reminded him.

"That's true, I did tell you that, but things change, Sophie." He shrugged.

"What things have changed?" she asked with a lift of her brow. A sudden dawning horror had her all but gaping at him. "Does this have anything to do with James?"

At least he had the good grace to flush. "Well, a little," he admitted. "Sophie, listen, the girls need a father—"

"The girls *had* a father, Max," she said quietly, setting her coffee down on the nightstand, the taste going bitter in her mouth. "He died. Three years ago. Remember?" she added quietly.

"Damn it, Sophie. I'm tired of pretending," he exploded, dragging a hand through his hair. Max reached for her hands, held them in his own. "Listen to me," he said, giving her hands a shake. "I can't pretend any longer. When I agreed to this arrangement with you and Michael, I did so because I believed Michael would be the girls' father in every sense of the word. For my brother, I could justify stepping aside to give him and you something you both wanted more than anything in the world— babies. And I don't regret it, Sophie, not one bit." He hesitated, trying to gather his composure. "But when we made this arrangement, none of us ever thought or even considered that Michael would die, and the girls would grow up fatherless. But he did and nothing we can do will change that. But as far as I'm concerned when Michael died that canceled our deal."

"You…you…can't mean that," Sophie whispered, her voice barely audible. Fear, stark and real beat with every pulse of her heart, threading its way through every part of her body.

Horrified and heartbroken by his statements, she tried to yank her hands from his, but he held on tight. He hadn't asked her to marry her because he loved her or wanted her for his wife, he was merely trying to protect his *parental* rights. By marrying her, he would insure that she wouldn't marry James. Or anyone else. This had nothing to do with his feelings for her, but was more of a preemptive strike so to speak.

She had no idea anything could hurt so much. She'd never expected this of Max.

"I damn well do mean it," Max snapped. "I stepped aside so my brother could be a father to those girls—*my* daughters," he clarified, realizing it was the first time he'd ever said the words aloud. "When you and Michael came to me and asked me about the artificial insemination, I agreed because I loved my brother and knew how desperately he was hurting, knew how the fact that he couldn't conceive was eating him alive. And with that agreement, Sophie, I knew full well that I was giving up all parental rights to *my* children and I did so willingly because I knew how much having children meant to Michael. And to you," he added.

"But at the time, Sophie, I never imagined I'd want a family of my own, not with my life and career. But the moment I saw those little babies something changed." Vaguely, Max gestured with his hand, not certain even he understood exactly what had happened. "I fell head over heels in love with them that day, Sophie, but I'd made a deal with you and my brother and I'm a man of my word. But I never counted on my brother dying, and leaving those little girls fatherless, let alone leaving them open to their mother marrying some other man who would step right in and become the father my brother was *supposed* to be. Maybe it's wrong, Sophie, but what I feel in my heart can't be wrong. I love those girls with my whole heart. They're *my* daughters,'' he reiterated firmly. ''And even though none of us planned for it, my brother is dead. These are the facts and we can't change them. The girls need a father, and I think it's about time someone acknowledges the fact that *I'm* their damn father.'' He rose, his gaze still locked on hers. ''Because if you think I'm going to step aside *again,* and let some other man become a father to my beloved *daughters,* you're sadly mistaken. I did it once, for my brother's sake, but never again.''

''Max.'' Tears spilled unheeded down Sophie's cheeks, tears of shock, of grief, and above all fear. ''Oh my God, Max, you can't mean that?'' she said, trying to think of all the enormous complications his statement could bring on.

''The hell I don't,'' Max said firmly, his voice as viciously sharp as a stiletto.

She began to tremble, every nerve in her body shaking in fear and disbelief. Her heart felt as though it had jumped to her throat, choking her.

''Don't cry, Sophie,'' Max ordered nervously. ''Please. Just don't cry.'' Near panicked by her tears, and by the way all of this had come out, Max began to pace. He had a feeling he'd blown it. Women didn't normally cry when you asked them to marry them.

Did they?

At least he didn't think they did, but what did he know. He'd never asked anyone to marry him before.

"I... I don't know what to say to you," she said, as tears dampened her cheeks. The tears were no match for the fear and grief swamping her. "I didn't ever expect anything like this to happen."

"Well hell, Sophie, to tell you the truth, neither did I," Max admitted, sinking down on the bed and trying to wrap his arms around her. She shook her head, then leaned back against the headboard, wiping her eyes, trying to think and hide her broken heart.

"Can I help it I fell in love with those two gorgeous little girls on sight?" A slight smile curved his lips as he remembered the day the twins were born; the day he first saw the girls, so small, so pink, so very helpless. They'd gotten a hold of his heart and had never let go. Knowing he'd never be able to claim them had chewed a giant-sized hole in his heart during the past six years.

It was the first time in his life he understood true heartbreak, but he had no choice. He'd made an agreement, and he had to honor it. Honor it and walk away from the two best things that had ever happened in his life.

It had almost killed him, something he'd never admitted to anyone.

Sophie sniffled. Max loved the girls, that was clear. It was his feelings—or rather lack of them—for her that were the problem.

"Max, I'm really and truly sorry. I know you love the girls and always have, and I know you'd do anything for them, but I can't marry you."

He felt her words stab him like a knife, quick and sharp right in the heart. It began to throb and ache as if an actual physical wound had been inflicted on him.

He'd never anticipated this. Never anticipated that she'd turn him down. Perhaps her relationship with Beardsley was a lot more serious than he'd anticipated or wanted to believe.

"Can't, Sophie?" he asked, trying to conceal his own breaking heart. "Or won't?"

She had no answer for him. None. She had no idea what to say to him, how to tell him that she wouldn't and couldn't marry him, not just for the girls' sake, not just to ensure his paternity.

If she ever married again—if—and that was a really big question now, she wanted all the things she'd never had with Michael. All the things she'd always dreamed about, the things that had eluded her for very long in her life.

Was it too much to want a man who loved you and only you, and married you because he wanted to spend his life with you?

That's all she'd ever wanted. But not just any

man. A man whom she could love just as much in return.

A man who would be a true father to her precious daughters, and while she had no doubt that Max would be an ideal father, she wasn't so certain about the husband part. If he wasn't asking her to marry him because he loved her, then their marriage had no chance.

She'd already been in a marriage where she was the only one who gave, who loved, who sacrificed and did all that she could to save her marriage, and she knew firsthand that one person couldn't make or save a marriage.

And she'd never go through that heartbreak and disappointment again. Not even for Max in spite of how much she loved him.

So she merely shook her head.

"Are you going to leave?" she asked softly, gripping the edge of the sheet so tightly in her hands her knuckles whitened.

"Do you want me to leave?" he asked carefully.

Finally, she forced herself to look at him. Her heart was beating a wicked, frightened tattoo against her chest at the thought of him leaving because this time she feared he might never come back.

"You promised the girls you'd be here for Thanksgiving," she said. "If you leave before that they'll be devastated and disappointed." It was the truth, she comforted herself, but little consolation knowing at the moment she simply couldn't face him leaving, not now, not after last night.

"Fine." The word snapped out of his mouth. "I'll stay through Thanksgiving." And then he had no idea what he would do or where he'd go. He had thought he'd be here, in his home, with Sophie and the girls. Forever. Apparently he'd been wrong.

"Good." Her words were just as sharp if a bit softer.

He stood up.

"Where are you going?"

"To take a shower," he snapped. "I've got things to do."

"Max?"

Her voice stopped him, but he didn't bother to turn around. "What?"

"Are you…are you going to say anything to the girls?" She had to take a breath, but it felt as if her lungs were constricted. "Are you going to tell them the truth? That you're their father?"

He turned to her and she could see the pain, the anguish in his eyes. She'd never realized how hard this had been for him, but then again, he'd walked away from his own children so that his brother could have a family.

"Sophie, what? I would never do anything to hurt the girls. Never." He hesitated a moment. "I'm still the same person I was before we had this conversation. Nothing's really changed, Sophie, I mean it's not like you didn't know I was the girls' biological father.''

"I know, but I guess I just never expected you to want to be a true father to the girls. I mean, being a father is an incredible responsibility, Max.''

He frowned. "I know that, Sophie.''

"And you don't exactly have a stellar history with staying in one place or settling down,'' she pointed out.

"I know that, too.'' Blowing out a breath, he dragged a hand through his hair. There was no point in telling her all the changes and adjustments he'd made in his life so he could stay in one place, so he could be a full-time father and a full-time husband.

What was the point?

She'd made it clear she didn't want to marry him.

"Sophie, I don't want to do anything to hurt you or the girls, or worse, to disrupt their lives.''

"I appreciate that, Max,'' she said solemnly.

"Sophie, this is me, remember?'' he said softly.

"I know, but this really changes things.'' She took a breath, let it out slowly. "What I don't want, Max, is for the girls to learn that you're their father, and then in a month or two have you get bored or tired of playing daddy or staying in one place and then get restless and feel the need to take off again for a year or two or three. I think that would be far more harmful to the girls than not having a father figure at all.''

"I agree with you, Sophie, and I promise you I won't do that." He glanced at her. "Like you, I only want what's best for the girls."

"I know," she said quietly. "And I appreciate it."

"Yeah, great," he said. "Look, I'd really like to go take my shower now before the girls get home."

"Fine." With her heart aching, Sophie watched him walk out of the room, knowing that in spite of what he said, nothing would ever be the same between them.

Nothing.

Chapter Nine

Furious with himself and the way things had gone, Max, like almost everyone else in and near the city of Chicago, spent the rest of Saturday and most of Sunday shoveling them out.

He shoveled the long driveway, the sidewalks, and then when he was done, frozen and exhausted, he looked for something else to do. Anything to keep him busy.

He was both embarrassed and feeling a tad stupid. How could he have blundered so badly? he wondered. He'd never expected Sophie to turn him down. Now, he wondered how he could have been so stupid and not even *considered* the possibility.

He didn't know.

By the time the girls and Carm returned home Sunday afternoon shortly after the trains resumed running again, he and Sophie were doing their best to avoid one another. Other than being civil to one another, he made himself scarce so he wouldn't have to face her. It was far too awkward. He was in the basement playroom doing things he'd already done ten times. Or out in the carriage house checking on the progress of the workmen, or up in his room, working at staying…busy.

By Sunday evening he was up in his room, nursing his broken heart and his severely sore shoulder.

He had a feeling shoveling snow for five and a half hours wasn't exactly what the doctor had in mind when he told him to rest his collarbone.

"Uncle Max?" Carrie and Mary stood in the doorway of his bedroom, watching as he worked on his laptop. He'd been fiddling around for a couple months with some of the photos he'd taken, photos of the girls from the time they were born. He'd been thinking about making a special photo album for Sophie for Christmas.

"Hi, girls," he said, looking up from his computer with a smile. "Did you guys have a good time downtown?" He leaned back and watched as they bounced into the room full of vibrant nerves and unending energy, anxious to share their adventure with him.

"We had a great time, Uncle Max," Mary said with a roll of her eyes as she hopped up on his bed and crossed her legs under her. "We ate in a hotel. I had a hot dog and French fries and a big, huge malt." She made a huge figure with her hand to indicate the size of her malt.

"Yeah, and I had a hot dog, two orders of fries and a strawberry malt," Carrie said, hopping up on the bed next to her sister. "What did you and Mama do while we were gone, Uncle Max?"

Max froze. "What...uh...did your mother and I, do?" he repeated nervously. He wasn't about to tell the girls he and Sophie had spent the night making mad, passionate love. "Well, I borrowed your sled to go pick up your mother from school."

"Our sled?" Mary bounced on her knees in excitement. "Did you really use our sled to pick Mama up from school?"

"Absolutely," Max confirmed with a grin, getting up and scooting the girls over a bit so he could join them. He slid an arm around each of them as he crossed his legs comfortably on the bedspread.

"Then what did you do?" Carrie asked.

"Then we had dinner." He glanced from one to the other. "It was kind of like a picnic, but indoors. Since we didn't have any power or lights or heat, I rigged up a makeshift grill in the fireplace and we cooked steaks and baked potatoes on it."

"Cool," Mary said, her eyes rounding as she

yawned. "Could we have an indoor picnic some-time, too, Uncle Max?" she asked, stifling another yawn.

"Sure, sweetheart. I don't think your mother would mind."

"Uncle Max? Are you still gonna pick us up from school tomorrow?" Carrie asked with a frown, rubbing the freckles on her nose. "Cuz we've got ballet practice, remember? For our recital. We have to be there by three-thirty and Mama won't be done by then."

"I'm supposed to pick you up and take you to practice, and then your mother will pick you up on her way home, right?" he said, pleased he remembered.

"Right, Uncle Max." Carrie rubbed her tummy. "It's Monday, Uncle Max," Carrie said, letting her voice trail off as she glanced at her sister. They exchanged a look. "We get our spelling quizzes back on Monday," she reminded him.

Every Monday night since he'd been there they had ordered pizza. The girls loved it and it gave Sophie a break from cooking, especially now when things were starting to get so hectic. With the girls' recital and the holidays coming up, he figured Sophie could use a night off.

"Yeah, I know," he said, shifting his weight. "And I seem to recall I promised you both that we could order pizza on Monday if you both did well on your spelling quiz, right?'' He'd made the Monday pizza ritual an incentive for the girls with their schoolwork.

Carrie and Mary grinned. ''That's right, Uncle Max.'' Carrie frowned a bit. ''I think I got an A,'' she said hesitantly. ''But I'm not sure.''

''Me, either,'' Mary chimed in with a frown of her own.

''Doing good on the quiz doesn't necessarily mean getting an A,'' Max said gently, knowing that spelling was difficult for Carrie, who'd been having a very hard time learning to spell. But she was working on it, he thought proudly, planting a kiss on the top of her head. ''Sweetheart, doing good merely means that you did your very best. That's all I'll ever ask or expect of you.'' He glanced at Mary. ''Of either of you.''

''Were you good in spelling, Uncle Max?'' Carrie asked, rubbing a fist against her tired eyes. He laughed.

''Uh, no, Carrie, I'm afraid I'm still not a very good speller.'' But then he'd never had anyone to study with him, help him, or encourage him. ''Thankfully, computers have spell-checkers on them, but I think because I'm not very good I have to work twice as hard when I write something, so I think it's important that you try to learn to spell now, when you're young.''

''Uncle Max, are you ever gonna tell us what

you're doing in the carriage house?'' Mary asked, abruptly changing the subject.

He laughed. ''Of course. But like I said it's a surprise.''

''For who?'' Carrie asked curiously.

''It's a surprise for your mother, sweetheart,'' he said quietly, his heart aching again. ''It's a surprise I planned for your mother.'' He thought about Sophie, about Saturday night, about how happy he'd been for a few, short blissful hours.

Thought too, about the fact that she didn't want to marry him, didn't want to be his wife or share her life with him. He glanced at the girls and his heart filled with love. At least he still had his daughters, he thought. But the thought brought on another sharp ache. Yes, he still had his daughters—for the moment—but he wanted, needed Sophie.

''Mama loves surprises,'' Carrie said, scooting closer to him.

''Yeah,'' Mary added. ''But are you going to tell us about it soon? We really want to know what's going on.''

''You'll know what the surprise is soon enough,'' he promised, realizing he'd never known when he'd asked Sophie to marry him, that the surprise would truly be on him.

''Uncle Max! Uncle Max!'' Waving her spelling quiz high in the air, Mary grinned as she watched Max pull into the circular drive in front of school.

Waving at her to let her know he'd spotted her, Max slowly eased the car to the curb, put it in park, then climbed out.

"Hi, sweetheart." He glanced around, then frowned. "Where's Carrie?" he asked worriedly, trying to pick Carrie out of the crowd of kids surging out the double doors of the school.

Mary shrugged. "Dunno." She waved her paper at him again. "I got an A on my quiz, Uncle Max." Bouncing up and down in excitement, her bright yellow snow boots made squeaky sounds against the packed snow and she nearly toppled over sideward. "I told ya."

He grinned, catching her up in a hug and then righting her again. "Yes, you did, sweetheart. Pizza all around tonight," he said, glancing beyond her and trying to find Carrie.

Max frowned. He didn't see Carrie. "Mary, when was the last time you saw Carrie?" Max asked with a scowl, opening the passenger door for her.

"In art class," she said, looking up at him.

"When was that?" he asked worriedly, glancing at his watch. Carrie knew she was supposed to meet him right here. They had to get to ballet practice. The girls weren't the kind of kids who disobeyed.

Mary shrugged. "Dunno. But while I was drawing someone came in to get her. She had to go to the office."

"The office," Max repeated with a scowl. "What for?"

"Dunno," Mary said with another shrug.

"Come on, sweetheart." He reached for her hand, helping her out of the car again. "Let's go find her."

"Okay."

"Do you know where the office is?"

"'Course." Mary shrugged again. "Everyone knows where it's at."

"Everyone except me," Max said, protecting Mary with his body as they pushed their way through the mass of kids, all going in the wrong direction.

"Don't worry, Uncle Max," Mary said, holding his hand tightly. "I'll take you there."

"And another thing, young lady," James said, standing over Carrie and glowering at her. "I understand food was found in your locker again." He shook his finger at her, making her cringe away from him. "How many times have you children been told that keeping food in your locker simply attracts bugs? Don't you ever listen to what you're told? How many times do I have to explain these things to you?" Shaking his head, he leaned over her, planting his hands on either side of the chair arms.

"Are you listening to me, young lady?" James

boomed, furious. "No wonder you can't remember not to put food in your locker. You don't listen, do you?"

"I listen," she whispered, staring at her shoes. "Honest. I do."

"You *don't* listen," he countered.

"I do," she whispered, daring to glance up at him. Her lip was trembling and her eyes were blurred by big, fat tears. "I do. Honest."

"Are you sassing me now?" he demanded, just as the door to his outer office opened.

Max, with Mary trailing right next to him, had heard Beardsley all the way out in the hall. He took one look at Carrie's tears and her terrified face, and swore under his breath.

"Come here, sweetheart," he said, going down on his haunches and opening his arms to Carrie. For the moment, he ignored Beardsley. He'd deal with him in a minute.

Carrie slithered out of the chair and away from Beardsley, running straight into her uncle's arms. She wrapped her skinny arms tightly around him and started to sob.

"He yelled at me again, Uncle Max," she sobbed in a whisper.

"I know, sweetheart, I heard it." The fact that James had caused him to break a solemn promise he'd made to his daughter, a promise he'd made about her safety and security only fueled Max's temper. "And I'm sorry, but I'll take care of it, baby, I promise." He wiped her tears. "Don't cry, baby," he soothed, glaring over her head at James. "Don't cry. It's over now. He's never going to scare you again. And this time I mean it."

As he held her shaking little body, anger unlike anything Max had ever known took hold. He lifted Carrie's chin and began to kiss her face.

"Don't cry, sweetheart," he crooned. "It's all right. Uncle Max is here. He won't yell at you anymore."

Sniffling, Carrie swiped the back of her hand against her drippy nose, then nodded. "Can we leave, Uncle Max?" she whispered, lifting her head and daring a glance back at Beardsley. "Please, Uncle Max. I want to go home now."

"In just a minute, sweetheart." He kissed her cheek, then turned to Mary. "Mary, would you please take your sister out to the car."

"Okay, Uncle Max," Mary said, taking Carrie's hand and glaring at Beardsley for making her sister cry. "But aren't you coming?" she asked worriedly.

"I'll be there in just a minute, honey." He kissed them both on the cheek, then stood up and walked them to the door, opening it for them. "Now go straight to the car. It's parked right out in front and it's not locked. I'll be right out."

"Are you sure you're gonna come?" Carrie whispered, crestfallen and still desolate.

"I promise, baby." He smiled at her, then gave her another quick hug. "I'll be right out."

Carrie nodded, cast one last glance back at Beardsley, shuddered, then followed her sister out the door and down the hall.

Letting out a slow, even breath in an effort to control himself, Max stood up.

"No wonder that child doesn't listen," James snapped, oblivious to the anger simmering in Max's eyes. "You spoil her."

"Do I?" Max asked, taking a step closer to Beardsley until he was forced to take a step back.

"What are you doing?" James asked nervously, practically bending backward over his desk.

"I warned you, didn't I?" Max said, his voice cold and lethal. "I gave you fair warning, but you didn't listen to me, now did you?"

"See here, now," James cautioned. "I'll call security if you come any closer."

"Good." Max grinned a moment before he fisted his hand. "That way you'll have someone to help you pick up your teeth." Without another word, Max let his fist fly, landing right smack dab in the middle of James's pompous, arrogant face.

"Rino, darling," Carm purred as she started the CD over again. "I'd like to try that new step again. The one you taught me last week."

Nodding, Rino stuffed his unlit cigar back in the

corner of his mouth and moved toward Carm. "Okay, doll, whatever you say."

They'd just started moving to the music when the phone rang. "Oh, I have to get that," Carm said. "Max is waiting for some delivery men." Pulling her earring off, and humming softly, Carm went to the phone to answer it.

"Hello."

"Uh… Mother, it's Sophie."

Carm's dark brows drew together. "Yes dear, after thirty years I recognize your voice," she said with a wry smile. Then, as she realized something was wrong, a shot of fear whisked through Carm and she sank down into a chair as her knees all but gave out. "Sophie, what is it?" she asked, her heart beating frantically. "What's wrong, dear? Has something happened to the children?"

"Uh, no, Mom, the girls are fine. But, Mom, I'm in trouble and I need your help."

"Sweetheart, don't worry," Carm said softly. "I'm here, dear, whatever it is, I'm here. Can you tell me exactly what's wrong?" Carm asked carefully as Rino stood before her, a concerned frown on his face. She reached for his hand and he held hers in comfort, patting it awkwardly while she talked. And listened.

"Well, Mother, Max is in jail and I need you to come and get the girls for me."

Stunned, Carm blinked, quickly trying to digest

everything. "I see, dear. Just tell me where you're at, dear, and Rino will bring me there immediately."

"I'm in the sheriff's office, Mom. I've got to post bail for Max."

"Bail?" Carm repeated dully. "Don't fret, dear. We'll be right there. Just hang on, darling, it shouldn't take us more than fifteen minutes." Carm slammed down the phone as Rino took her hands.

"You okay, doll?" he asked worriedly, talking around the unlit stogie.

"Yes, dear, but we have to go down to the sheriff's office to get the girls."

"Someone locked up your little girls?" he repeated with a scowl. "Who?" he scowled. "Just tell me who did this," he demanded, insulted for her and ready to right the wrong. "And I'll take care of it."

"Thank you, dear, but that's not necessary. It's not the girls who are locked up, but Max," she said.

"They locked up Max?" Rino repeated with another scowl. "What the heck did he do?"

"I don't know, dear," Carm said, hurrying to the closet to get her coat. "But I think we're about to find out."

"Grandma! Grandma!" Mary raced to her grandmother who caught her in a hug. "Guess what? Uncle Max popped Mr. Beardsley right smack dab in the face." Grinning proudly, Mary did a pantomime of punching herself in the nose and nearly knocked herself down in the process. Her grandmother caught her shoulders to right her.

"Really, dear?" One brow lifted and Carm glanced at Rino. "How very...exciting." She took Mary's hand. "Where's your mother, dear?"

"Over there." Mary pointed. "Mr. Beardsley yelled at Carrie and made her cry. Again," Mary said with a shake of her head.

"Who yelled at your sister?" Rino boomed, glancing around for the offender.

"Mr. Beardsley," Mary said.

Slipping her hand in his, Mary looked up at him and said, "He yelled at Carrie again and she cried. So Uncle Max popped him one."

"Well, good for him, then," Rino said.

"Rino, dear," Carm cautioned with a smile and he hung his head.

"Sorry, doll." He glanced down at Mary. "It's not good to hit people, honey. Not unlessing they deserve it," he added firmly.

"Sophie." Spotting her daughter pacing the outer office floor, Carm hurried toward her and enfolded her in a quick hug. "Mary told us what happened."

"Hi, doll," Rino said, giving Sophie a smile and a hug. "Don't worry, everything's going to be okee-dokee." He reached in his pants pocket and pulled out a wad of bills the size of a baseball, pressing them into Sophie's hand. "Here. Take this. Use whatever you need for bail money. I got more if you need it.''

Sophie's eyes widened at the fistfull of money. There had to be thousands and thousands of dollars here and he was simply handing it to her.

''Rino,'' she said, a catch in her voice. ''Thank you, really, but I don't need it,'' she said, leaning forward to kiss his cheek and press the bills back into his hand. A retired contractor who'd built most of the schools in the area, Rino was a short, squat man with arms and legs the size of tree trunks. He was also the sweetest, gentlest man and her mother adored him. And with good reason, Sophie thought with a grateful smile. ''They're going to release Max on his own recognizance.''

''You're sure?'' he asked doubtfully, trying to hand the money back to her. ''Cuz really, I don't need it. I got lots more.''

''Honest.'' Sophie smiled at him. ''But thank you for offering.''

He flushed, and hung his head again. ''Ah, it's nothing.'' He glanced at her mother and she could see the love and adoration in his eyes. ''You're the doll's daughter. There ain't nuthin' I wouldn't do for her.'' He grinned at Sophie. ''Or for you or your kids.''

Sophie and her mother exchanged looks, and for the first time in a long time Sophie saw that dreamy look of love in her mother's eyes. She hadn't seen that look, not through any of her mother's other marriages or relationships, not since her father had died.

But it was back, and Sophie couldn't help but feel overjoyed for her mother. And for Rino.

"Thank you, Rino." Impulsively, Sophie kissed him again. Embarrassed, his wrinkled face flushed beet-red.

"What can we do, dear?" Carm asked, glancing around to find Carrie. She was huddled on a chair, her eyes and nose red from crying. "The poor little thing. Look at her."

Sophie let out a long breath. "I don't really want the girls here any longer than they have to be, Mother." Sophie glanced up at the wall clock. "They've already missed their ballet class, and Carrie's really been frightened."

"Don't worry, dear. Rino and I will take the girls home and get them settled in." She smiled, grateful she was able to help, to contribute. "Then how about if we order a pizza and rent a movie for them? That ought to take their mind off all the excitement today."

Sophie glanced across the room at her daughter and felt her heart ache. The poor little thing. She had a feeling it would take more than a pizza and movie to erase the fear and the memory from Carrie's mind. Her anger at James grew and Sophie tried to bank it down and concentrate on what was important at the moment. Her daughters. And Max.

"That would be wonderful, Mom," Sophie said, kissing her mother's cheek. She glanced at Rino. "Do you mind?" she asked him and he grinned.

"Mind spending the night with three beautiful women?" He grinned. "All men should be so lucky." He turned, spotted Carrie and let his smile go wider. He knelt down and opened his arms wide. "Where's my little Carrie?" he called, his voice booming loudly through the outer office of the sheriff's office

"I'm right here, Mr. Rizzo," Carrie managed in just barely a whisper, smiling for the first time since she'd left Mr. Beardsley's office. She climbed down off the chair then ran straight into the warmth and protection of Rino's big arms.

With his booming laugh, he hauled her up and on his hip. "So, doll, what do you say?" He rubbed his tummy. "I'm real hungry. I got a hankering for pizza. And lots of it," he added, smacking his lips loudly and making Carrie giggle. "How about you?" he asked and Carrie nodded, winding her arms around his neck. "Maybe with some cheese sticks and a couple of hot dogs and French fries on the side. What do you think?"

"Could we maybe get extra cheese?" Carrie whispered, smiling at her mother and grandmother as Mr. Rizzo took her sister's hand and began walking toward the door with them.

"Doll, we can get anything you want." He

pressed a loud, smacking kiss to Carrie's cheek, then grinned at her. "Anything you want, doll, anything at all."

"Could we maybe get some brownies for dessert?" Mary asked, holding his hand tight.

"We can get a dozen of 'em. For each of us," he added with a laugh.

"That's too many," Carrie said with a whispered giggle, waving to her mother over his shoulder.

"Well, we're gonna stop and get some movies, too. How about that?" he asked, hiking Carrie up higher.

"Can we get *The Little Mermaid?*" Carrie asked, her eyes wide. "That's my favorite."

"You can get *The Little Mermaid* and anything else you want."

"How 'bout a puppy?" Mary asked slyly. "Can we maybe get a puppy on the way home?"

Rino looked at her and let loose a big, booming laugh. "A puppy, huh? Maybe. Just maybe we can," he considered with a grin as he pushed open the double doors and led the girls out in the hallway to wait for their grandmother.

"Mom, thank you," Sophie said, touching her mother's arm. "I don't know what I'd have done without you and Rino today."

Carm's smile was dreamy. "He's a wonderful man, dear. Just like Max." Her mother hesitated, "You know, after your father died I never thought

I'd find love again, but I did.'' She patted Sophie's cheek. "You've found it too, darling, I just hope you realize and recognize it before it's too late.''

Max paced in his holding cell, rubbing his sore knuckles, wondering how Carrie was. He didn't regret punching Beardsley one bit, not one little bit.

He was just sorry he hadn't done it sooner.

The idea that Beardsley had scared Carrie so badly still angered him. He'd given him fair warning, he reasoned, but he had a feeling Sophie wasn't going to see it quite that way.

Max sighed, sinking down on the thin bunk. Sophie. He had no idea what to do about her. If she was upset with him before, he had no idea how she'd feel toward him now.

Well, he thought, morosely, Thanksgiving was in a week. If worse came to worst, he'd move into a hotel until then. He'd promised the girls he'd spend Thanksgiving with them and he intended to honor his promise.

"McCallister?'' A guard dressed in a perfectly pressed beige uniform with a key ring jiggling loudly at his waist stopped in front of his cell. "You're free to go.''

Max grabbed his coat. "Thanks.''

The guard unlocked the door and swung it open. "Try to stay outta trouble, will you?'' the guard said with a bored expression. "All this paperwork puts a crimp in my day,'' he complained as Max swept past him and headed out of the holding cell area.

"Max.'' Sophie rushed to him, so relieved to see him she couldn't believe it. She threw her arms around him and simply hung on. "I was so worried, so scared.''

"I'm surprised to see you here,'' Max said.

"Why?'' she asked in alarm. "Why on earth wouldn't I be here?''

He sighed. "Because I decked James, and I won't apologize for it, Sophie. I warned him,'' he added, his voice growing with fury. "I gave him fair warning about yelling at the girls.'' Max shook his head, his eyes narrowed and glittering. "When I walked in his office and saw Carrie cowering in fear, tears in her eyes, I couldn't believe it.'' Max shook his head, blowing out a frustrated breath. "No matter what happens, Sophie, I am never going to let anyone scare, threaten or intimidate my daughters. Not now. Not ever.''

"Max.''

"And another thing,'' he went on, pulling her down next to him in the nearest empty chairs, figuring he might as well get all this out in the open now. "I know this is probably going to put a crimp in your relationship with Beardsley and I'm sorry, but I'm not about to sit back and let some guy scare my kids, no matter what your relationship or involvement with him. Someone has to protect those girls and I think a father not only has a right, but a responsibility to do that, and that's what I intend to do whether you like it or not. So we'd better get that straight right here and now. You may not want to marry me, Sophie, but that doesn't mean I'm not going to be a father, a *real* father, to my daughters and a major part of their life each and every day. I think I've earned that right, Sophie, but that doesn't mean I'll interfere in your life any more than I have to. I told you the night I got here that I was thinking about making some changes in my life, and I've got most of them set in motion. In January I'm going to be joining the faculty of the local community college, and my lawyer has just about finished negotiations for the sale of two books. The first will be a glossy, high-end coffee table book of the photographs I've taken over the years, and the second will be a book about all my adventures taking those photographs, so I'm going to be right here for the foreseeable future, being a daily part of the girls' lives. Now, I'm sure you want me to leave, so I'll go back to the house and pack my stuff and move into a hotel until Thanksgiving, but I told the girls I'd be here for Thanksgiving and I intend to keep that promise, not just this Thanksgiving, but every Thanksgiving.''

''Max?''

''What?'' he asked glancing at her.

''Shut up.'' She pressed her lips to his to quiet him. Startled, his eyes widened and he drew back from her, refusing to hope, refusing to allow himself to be rejected again.

Sophie took a deep breath. ''Max, do you know why I said I wouldn't marry you?''

He looked at her, wondering if this was supposed to be some kind of trick question. ''Yeah,'' he said glumly, ''because of Beardsley. Right?''

''Max.'' She laid a hand on his arm, stopping him so she could turn and face him. Her eyes widened in alarm as his words registered. ''Do you think that's why I turned down your marriage proposal, because of *James?*'' she asked, her voice edging upward in shock.

''Of course,'' he said with a shrug. ''That night I tried to talk to you about it, but you wouldn't talk about it with me.''

''Max.'' Tears filled her eyes. ''I didn't want to talk about James because I wanted you to kiss me,'' she admitted softly. ''I turned you down, Max, not because of James, but because when a man asks a woman to marry him, it's not usually just for their children's sake.''

He blinked at her. *Their* children. She'd never referred to the girls that way. His heart began to hope. ''Our children?''

She nodded. ''You see, when I turned you down it was because I don't want you to marry me because of the girls. That would be for all the wrong reasons.

I wanted you to ask me to marry you because you loved me,'' she said, brushing at her tears.

He frowned. ''But Beardsley said that you and he had talked, were planning a weekend away so you could consider your future—''

''As you've repeatedly pointed out, Max, the man's an idiot,'' she snapped, her anger at James surfacing again.

''An idiot?'' One brow lifted. ''Are you telling me you didn't turn down my proposal because of Beardsley?'' he asked, confused.

''Max, I turned you down when you asked me to marry you because you asked me for the girls' sake, so the girls would have a father.''

''Well, yeah, of course. I think it's time for the girls to have a father, their real father—''

''But you never said a word about how you felt about me,'' she interrupted softly. He merely stared at her, stupefied.

''What?''

''You never said a word about how you felt about me, Max,'' she said. ''Generally, when a man asks a woman to marry him it's because he's in love with her.'' She managed to look at him. ''At least that's the norm. Now I know that nothing between us has ever been normal because of the circumstances.''

She took a breath, then closed her eyes for a moment. ''Max, I love you,'' she finally said when she opened her eyes. ''I've been in love with you for a very long time. And not like a friend or even my brother-in-law. I love you the way a woman loves a man. Totally. Completely and with my whole heart,'' she said softly, tears stinging her eyes.

''Sophie.'' His heart seemed to do a wild leap, then spin before settling back down in his chest. He slid his arms around her, held her close for a moment. ''I don't believe it.'' He drew back. ''I can't believe I didn't tell you how I felt about you. I love you, Sophie, not just because you're the mother of my children, not for any other reason except because you're you.'' He saw the joy in her eyes and felt it seep into his soul. ''Will you marry me, Sophie? Because I'm wildly, madly in love with you.'' He pressed his forehead to hers and let out a breath of relief. ''And will you be my wife forever, and make a home and a family with me and our daughters?''

''Just our daughters?'' she asked mischievously. It took a moment for her meaning to set in. Then he laughed and picked her up, swinging her around in joy.

''Our daughters. Our sons. As many children as you want.'' The thought of more children, more babies of his own to love, to cherish, to *father* was just about the icing on the cake.

She looked at him and felt all the years of longing and wanting and yearning melt away. ''Yes, Max.'' She threw her arms around him. ''Definitely, yes. I'll marry you and have more of your babies.''

Closing his eyes, Max held her tightly, ignoring the sheriff's deputies who were changing shifts and giving them suspicious looks.

"I love you, Sophie," he said softly. "More than anything in the world. And I'll try to remember to tell you each and every day." He grinned. "I love you so much, Sophie, that...well, you know that old carriage house out back of the house?"

"Yeah." She frowned. "The one you asked me if you could rent?"

He grinned. "I just needed a way to keep you outta there for a while."

"Why?" she asked, confused, and he sighed.

"Because, Sophie, you've given up so many of your dreams for everyone else, out of love for everyone else, well, the girls and I wanted to give you one of your dreams."

"A run-down carriage house?" she said with a laugh.

"Not exactly." Eyes shining in excitement, Max pulled out a wrinkled colored photo he'd been carrying around in his pocket since the night he'd arrived and handed it to her.

"What's this, Max?"

"It's a picture of your brand-new catering kitchen."

Slowly, she lifted her eyes to his. "Wh-what?"

He draped an arm around her shoulder. "Sophie, I worked it all out with an architect. It should be finished in about another week or ten days, but we totally tore the place apart and rebuilt it into a thoroughly modern catering kitchen. You'll have the latest in modern appliances, equipment, and anything and everything else you need." Rocking back on his heels, he grinned. "I've even hired you a full-time kitchen manager."

"A kitchen manager?" she repeated dully, trying to take all of this in. Her gaze studied his and she grinned. "My mother? You hired my mother?"

"You said she taught you to cook and is the one person who encouraged and inspired you. So I figured it was a dream you two could share, together."

Tears filled her eyes and Sophie stared at the beautiful picture, then lifted her gaze to Max. "I don't know what to say," she stammered, her voice catching. "This...this is all like a dream come true."

"Well, Sophie, you've been making everyone else's dreams come true in lieu of your own, so I think it's about time someone made yours come true."

"Max." She laid her head on his shoulder and simply inhaled his scent. "I love you more than anything in the world."

"And I love you, Sophie."

Resting her head on his shoulder, she slid her arm around his waist and held on to his security, his stability, his love. "Let's go home, Max. To our children."

He grinned. Home. He knew home was with Sophie and the girls all along.

"Yeah, Sophie, let's go home." Arm in arm they walked out of the police station and into their future together.

Epilogue

*Thanksgiving
One Year Later*

"Daddy? How come we're going to Grandma and Grandpa Rino's for turkey day?" Carrie asked as she scrambled up into her father's lap so he could buckle her black patent-leather dress shoes. "How come we're not going to have turkey day here like we always do?"

Nuzzling her, Max wrapped one arm around his daughter as he buckled her shoes. "Well, honey, since this is Grandma and Grandpa Rino's first Thanksgiving in their new house—"

"You mean since they gots married?" Carrie asked, and Max nodded.

"That's right, honey," he said with a smile. "Since they got married. And remember how Mama and I explained that since Mama's going to have our new baby any day now—"

"Mama says any second now," Mary injected with a roll of her eyes as she came bounding down the stairs clutching the orange-and-brown-paper Thanksgiving turkey she'd made in school to take to her grandmother's house.

Max laughed, reaching out an arm to snag his other daughter and pull her into his lap, as well, checking her patent-leather shoes to make sure they were buckled. "Remember what I told you, girls?"

Carrie's head bobbed up and down. "That Mama's big and uncomfortable, and until the baby is born she's probably going to be…cranky?" Carrie asked, screwing her brows up as she tried to remember exactly what her father had said. "So we should be nice and help her as much as possible."

"Exactly," Max said with a smile, making Carrie beam that she'd remembered. "So, this year, Grandma's going to make Thanksgiving dinner."

"And next year," Mary said excitedly, bouncing on her father's lap, "we'll have turkey day here—"

"With and our new brother or sister, right, Daddy?" Carrie finished, and Max nodded, almost as excited as his daughter at the prospect. He'd missed so much of the girls' early years that the prospect of being here full-time for his next child, of having all of his children and his whole family together for the holidays and celebrating the way normal families did, brought more joy to his heart than he ever thought possible.

"Max?"

"There's your mama now, girls," Max said, setting the girls down on the couch. "Let me go help her down the stairs.

"You look beautiful, Sophie," Max said with a grin as he went up the stairs to take Sophie's hand. She was big and ungainly and she'd never looked more beautiful to him.

"Yeah, well, tell that to someone who doesn't need a crane to get from one place to the other." Rubbing her belly, Sophie took Max's hand and slowly made her way down the stairs.

Max laughed, bringing her hand to his lips for a kiss. "The girls made a beautiful centerpiece for your mother's table," he said proudly as Mary waved her paper turkey in the air as if it were about to take flight.

"Yeah, well, I think we have to make a stop before we head to my mother's."

"A stop," Max said, opening the closet door to get Sophie's coat. He stopped abruptly when he saw the look on her face. The coat slipped from his fingers. "Oh, no." He went white. "Now?" He tried to keep the panic from his voice.

Sophie rubbed her tummy again and sighed. "I'm afraid so, Max." She managed a smile as another labor pain sliced through her. "I think we'd better stop at the hospital first."

For a moment, Max merely stood there frozen. Then he went into action. "Girls, remember what we practiced? Now's the time," he said, giving orders like a drill sergeant. "Mary, you go get your mother's and the baby's suitcase from the kitchen. Carrie, you call Grandma. The phone number is right by the phone, like we practiced."

"Daddy?" Carrie stood in front of him, looking at him wide-eyed. "What are you going to do?"

Sophie laughed. "Daddy's going to sit down for a minute," she said, giving Max a gentle nudge so he'd do exactly that on the bottom step of the stair. "Put your head between your legs for a minute, Max. And breathe, honey. Just breathe."

"But the baby—"

"The baby's not going anywhere." She smiled to try to ease the stark terror in his eyes. "Sit." He sat for a moment, taking several deep breaths to get his bearings back and calm himself.

"I got your suitcase, Mama," Mary said as she raced back from the kitchen, knocking the suitcase against her knees.

"And I called Grandma. They're going to meet us at the hospital," Carrie said.

Sophie leaned down to look into Max's face. "You okay, Daddy?" she asked, trying not to grin as she laid a hand along his cheek, her love for him filling her heart. This man who'd dodged bullets and who-knew-what-else during his career was intimidated by the mere thought of her giving birth. It was adorable.

"Yeah." Clearing his throat, Max nodded, and stood, wishing his legs were a bit steadier. "Yeah, I'm fine." He slung an arm around Sophie's shoulder. "I've waited a very long time for this day, Sophie. A long time to be a father, and a husband and have a family. My own family." Emotions swamped him. "You've given it to me, Sophie. All of it." He kissed her forehead. "I love you."

"I love you, too, sweetheart, but unless you want to add baby delivery as a new skill to your résumé we'd better get a move on."

He grinned suddenly, then glanced down at the girls. "Girls, let's go have our baby."

As it turned out, it wasn't one baby. It was two. Identical twin boys. Other than being disappointed the babies were bald, the girls were ecstatic since they were certain their mother arranged the double birth so they'd each have their own brother to play with and spoil.

As dusk fell over another Thanksgiving, Max relaxed contentedly in a chair next to Sophie's hospital bed while the girls played quietly on the floor and the newest additions to their family slept contentedly in the nursery.

"Daddy? I didn't get to use my Thanksgiving centerpiece," Mary said, rubbing her tired eyes with her fist as she climbed up onto her father's lap.

"That's okay, sweetheart," Max said, wrapping his arms around his daughter. "We can put it on our kitchen table when we bring Mama and your brothers home."

"But it won't be Thanksgiving any longer," Carrie complained. Max merely smiled, reaching for her and pulling her into his arms.

"Actually, sweetheart, as far as I'm concerned, every day we're all together is a day of thanksgiving."

And Max knew as he settled back in the chair, content with his wife by his side, his new babies in the nursery, and his daughters in his arms, that home wasn't just a place, it was something forever in your heart.

*   *   *   *   *

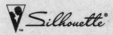

SPECIAL EDITION™

This January 2005...don't miss
the next book in bestselling author

Victoria Pade's

brand-new miniseries...

Northbridge Nuptials

Where a walk down the aisle is never far behind.

HAVING THE BACHELOR'S BABY

(SE #1658)

After sharing one incredible night in the arms of
Ben Walker, Clair Cabot is convinced she'll never
see the sexy reformed bad boy again. Then fate
throws her for a loop when she's forced to deal
with Ben in a professional capacity. Should she
also confess the very personal secret that's
growing in her belly?

Available at your favorite retail outlet.

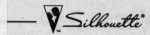

From

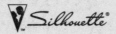

SPECIAL EDITION™

Patricia Kay

presents her next installment of

A dynasty in the baking...

HIS BEST FRIEND

(January 2005, SE #1660)

When wealthy Claudia Hathaway laid eyes on
John Renzo, she was blown away by his good
looks and sexy charm. He mistakenly gave her
the wrong contact information and so was gone
forever...or so she thought. The next thing she
knew, she was dating his cousin and caught
in a love triangle!

Available at your favorite retail outlet.

If you enjoyed what you just read,
then we've got an offer you can't resist!

Take 2 bestselling
love stories FREE!

Plus get a FREE surprise gift!

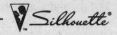

SPECIAL EDITION™

Don't miss the latest heartwarming tale from new author

Mary J. Forbes!

Ex-cop Jon Tucker was doing just fine living by his lonesome. Until his alluring new neighbor moved in next door, reminding him of everything he thought he'd left behind—family, togetherness, love. In fact, single mother Rianne Worth had awakened a yearning inside him so sweet he was hard-pressed to resist…especially when giving in to her meant becoming a family man, again.

A FATHER, AGAIN

Silhouette Special Edition #1661
On sale January 2005!

Only from Silhouette Books!